AF207382

A Wasp at a Funeral

A Wasp at a Funeral

Shelby Renjifo

Acknowledgments

Mama Bear, thank you for encouraging me to follow my dreams; without your constant strength, optimism, and patience, I wouldn't be the woman or writer I am today. Dad, thank you for calling me "a success" before I ever truly felt like one. My brother, Craig, thank you for your constant love and support. Thank you to all my close friends for always supporting my writing endeavors. Thank you to my Uncle David for encouraging me to extend this little tale in the first place and for all your help along the way. Thank you, Alexandra Milchan, for believing in me and giving me the extra push I needed with my story. Thank you to Emerson College for acknowledging my original short story, "A Wasp at a Funeral," as a nomination for the 37th Annual EVVY Awards Ceremony; this truly gave me the incentive to expand my work. Thank you to my professors at Emerson College for making me a better writer and inspiring me every day. A huge thank you to my mom, Laurie Giambrone, and Andrew Ferguson for reading various drafts and providing invaluable feedback for my piece. Thank you Lisalotte Crampton for working with me to bring this kickass book illustration to life. Thank you Vicki Janik and Tierney Bailey for your fantastic editorial skills; your guidance and feedback made all the difference. Neil Young and The Carpenters, your songs "Old Man" and "Close to You" truly molded my characters; music has been and always will be my guiding light for storytelling and I thank you both for your songs' inspirations.

To my dear uncle, William Daniel Sweeney,
and to all of those without a voice

"As the tears scald and start;
You shall love your crooked neighbor
With your crooked heart."
—W.H. Auden, "As I Walked Out One Evening"

PART I:

A WASP AT A FUNERAL

I could stand at the podium and say that Wesbrooke—my son—was a fine young man. I'd pause, look around, shed a tear. I could stand at the podium and say that my son—whom we called Brookes—was a fighter. He fought the good fight that is this cruel, unrelenting life filled with endless temptations—ugh, that may be a bit much. I could stand at the podium and say that my baby—Wesbrooke—with the sun in his eyes and the future waving proudly, brought only honor to his family with his diligence, lion-hearted nature, and beaming charisma. I could say all of this.

I sit dutifully in the church pew, front and center, between my husband, Joel, and my ex-husband, Wes. I feel acutely aware of my body and surroundings beneath my veneer of complacency. Look ahead, straighten your back—good. Now adjust your sleeve, breathe, blink—*buzzzz*. I break out of my reverie and glance around though no one else is daunted.

"Elizabeth, are you alright?" Wes asks.

I gather myself, nodding politely with a tight smile.

It's a funny question, asking someone if they're "alright," Wes. Being "alright" is a state of contentedness. Being "all right" means you are correct. A mother's intuition is said to be all right. But I'm a mother; I'm not all right. Nor am I alright, Wes.

I observe two portraits near my boy's casket: a young Wesbrooke Dodge Ellison IX and an even younger Wesbrooke Dodge Ellison IX. When I look at little Brookes, I see a smile bright with the notion that time wasn't to be feared, but revered in its spontaneity and indirect clarity of the moment and eternal life—there I go again. To hell with that damn podium. The truth is, his smile was an unaware smile— those are always the best kind—beautifully crooked in its lack of an understood perfection. I glance over at older Brookes and I flinch; I'm confused. His smile doesn't match his eyes. Glassy, lifeless: my son is a taxidermy human. I recognize his smile but someone replaced his eyes.

Bright blue. Brookes's eyes were bright blue. I remember when they hid behind a pair of round-rimmed glasses. Wes insisted the glasses emitted an heir of "European sophistication." I thought Brookes looked like Harry Potter and so did his entire third grade class. The glasses lasted a week because I broke them. The nanny saw me do it too—she'd been with us since Brookes was a newborn—and she nodded at me in understanding. But I didn't understand. Why did Brookes run to her first with the news? I told Wes we had to let her go; I saw her break Brookes's glasses and what were we to do about that sort of inappropriate, coddling?

The glasses lasted a week but the name stuck—Harry Potter. For years it stayed with him, because kids are relentless. And he cried— tears spilled behind every new pair of glasses. And he hardened—I was no longer Mommy, I was Mom, in harsh, brisk tones. I used to read those *Harry Potter* books to him before bed every night. Eight o'clock sharp was our nightly ritual.

"Mommy," said young Brookes shyly.

"Yes, doll."

"I know you need quiet time but can we start Harry early tonight?"

Let's start at 7:30 … 7:00 … 6:30 … let's keep going until I can start all over again with you, Brookes.

I spot some of his old classmates here. They're with their parents, whom I know from the Piping Rock Club. I watched them grow alongside my son. Over time, the Harry Potter jokes became nothing more than a playful jest on old times. Brookes's sensitivity morphed into a quick-witted, self-deprecating sense of humor; he grew a few inches; he played a little sports; he popped his shirt collar. He was in. But he was different. They were all very polite children, smart and inquisitive about the world, until their sense of self-entitlement set in. I look around and wonder when and how that complex forms.

I remember Piping's annual Fourth of July party the summer before Brookes's senior year of high school. Brookes and his friends, a sea of Vineyard Vines and sunglass tans, strolled up to the club's lawn before the fireworks display. I stood near the bar with Joel and some of the other parents. Brookes spotted me and gallantly ran over, planting a giant kiss on my cheek. I smiled proudly but I saw through his empty affection. Everything he did felt staged, very forced. He acted as if he was the title character in his own movie—the lovable yet wisecracking, cheesy popular kid in an 80s teen rom-com. I could see right past his façade—mother's intuition, I suppose. I encouraged it nevertheless, smiling endearingly as he made small talk with the others.

His friends kept walking. I felt daggers of envy in their parents' eyes. I soaked it up. I couldn't be more proud of my son as he eloquently discussed his final chapter ahead. Suddenly, blood trickled from his nose, staining his white, pristine polo and my pride. He didn't notice and kept talking, almost a mile a minute now.

"Honey, your—" I began.

Brookes now gathered himself quickly, covering his running nose.

The other parents threw cool side-glances at each other.

"Easy there, bud. Blood stains almost never come out," Joel cautioned good-naturedly. Then with a feigned casualness, he handed Brookes a napkin.

"Oops, thanks, Papa Joel," Brookes replied facetiously.

He squeezed his nose with the napkin, stuttering as he continued to make a joke of the matter. He then politely excused himself and headed back toward his friends.

"Not another nosebleed—ugh, ever since he was a child," I lied.

Buzzzzzzzz.

My entire body twitches with the abrupt noise. It sounds like a bumblebee. What if someone's allergic? A death at a funeral—a death at my *son's* funeral, I can't have that. I can't handle that—oh, that's right, I remind myself, bumblebees are harmless. It's the wasps you have to watch out for.

I curiously peered out my dorm window to the sound of raucous music and cheers down Beacon Street; a car-filled with rallying Harvard boys zoomed past. Today was their homecoming game against Yale, so naturally, these privileged Neanderthals had to make a city-wide spectacle of it. Meanwhile, I proudly tightened the purple and gold ribbons around my sleek, blonde, ponytail—Emerson's school colors. A collection of silky ribbons hung neatly along a rack near my combination desk and makeshift vanity; my roommate and best friend, Stacey Davies, always poked fun at this rather girlish habit. You can take the gal out of Sudbury, Mass, but you can't take Sudbury, Mass, out of the gal.

"That's the whitest shit I've ever seen," Stacey pointed to my ribbons on move-in day, "but all to their own, Bizzy Lizzie—cool if I call you that?"

I was to accompany Stacey to a Harvard tailgate, to my stark reluctance. There was a boy involved—as there always is—and when you met a Harvard guy, you kept him. But I knew this young man's prototype—with his life laid out on mom and dad's china platter: boarding school, college, trust fund … West Palm Beach. In other words—utterly predictable. On the flipside, Stacey was a flourishing thespian; with every performance, if you asked her for the world, she'd give you the universe. When she approached that stage, she revealed herself like the sun after a long, dark winter; I suppose when you spend your entire life as the source of your own light, your reflection beams back at you. She'd be someone—not just somebody. Put simply, her beau had quite a woman on his hands, and he had better know it.

As an art school student, I could not unravel the novelty of a first date at such a barbaric—dare I say, meathead—sports event. Therefore, he had one strike—as the football referee would decree.

But as a playwrighting major, I knew a thing or two about irony. So I smirked back at my arts and crafts project—a complimentary college shirt turned customized, cropped tee reading:

Emerson

Football

Undefeated Since 1880

We barely had a baseball team.

As I admired my handiwork, Stacey stormed in, donning a Harvard crew neck, khaki pants—and a giant pair of black platform combat boots. I didn't blink an eye; she was always trying new, niche looks. However, her tight, fashionably untamed curls, as big and bold as this era, now hung in dark, silky, mid-length waves. I didn't realize she was going to the salon for a blowout today—she looked fabulous.

"Your hair!" I hollered in excited surprise.

"Boots!" She frantically spouted. I had never seen her so frazzled. "I gotta do something about these boots."

"Yes, please. You look like a preppy dominatrix." I joked—I have always cherished our brutal honesty.

"Not today! Can I borrow these?"

She gestured to my brown riding boots sitting near my wardrobe.

"Of course ..." I responded, though this attire was far too functional for her taste.

I realized she had yet to take note of my masterpiece, as I popped up, goofily twirling around our forced-double. "And me? When will I find *my* Harvard man?!"

Stacey finally turned to me, gawking at my mid-afternoon impulse creation. Her signature, hearty laughter surely rang over the Esplanade and back.

"When Emerson sports makes a rank!" she squawked.

She plopped at my desk chair, fixated on my rainbow ribbon collection now.

"Any crimson?"

"Ohh," I teased, "we've moved to the dark side!"

"Nah, this is still white as hell."

I spotted Harvard's crisp red shade, and gently slid it off my rack.

"Got it!"

But as I reached for her hair, she impulsively grabbed my wrist. I flinched back, caught off guard, but quickly aware of my obtrusion.

"Sorry, go ahead," she quickly recomposed, breaking into a silly, snobby drawl to lighten back the mood, "style me proper, madam!"

As I lifted her new silky locks into a high pony, it jerked slightly. It was a wig.

"Oops! Didn't realize." I set a few bobby pins along her hairline for good measure.

"Hey, good!"

We laughed as I finished tying.

"All wrapped up in a pretty bow." She sing-songed at our reflections in perfect vibrato. "Well la-tee-daaaa!"

When I was seven, my mother took me to a doll store near our old summer home in Nantucket. The shop was enormous, with a wide range of beautiful, intricate, antique figures. In other words, it was a little girl's dream. I wandered around the place, in overwhelmed awe of these little masterpieces. My mother was busy chatting with the storeowner, an old friend of hers, but I didn't mind. There was so much to take in. Beyond the frilly dresses and delicate curlicue locks, there was one doll that kept catching my eye. She was in a glass encasement, sitting on a rocking chair in an eighteenth century-style kitchen. She wore a simple housedress and a brightly colored head wrap; the head wrap hid her hair but fully exposed her unique features. The doll was Black. I thought she was beautiful. I brought my mother over to the encasement. She stifled a laugh and called the storeowner over. I was embarrassed. I didn't understand.

"Come on now, let's find you a proper doll, honey," my mother said.

I understood.

Stacey and I strutted out of the Emerson dorms, followed by a ton of laughs and a handful of shirt commissions—and into the Harvard stadium parking lot, met with imminent stares and sharp whispers. We were in foreign yet too-familiar territory. Stacey took a deep breath.

"A Black girl and a feminist walk into a Harvard tailgate …" she joked quietly in my ear.

Before I could provide a sufficient punchline, Stacey bolted across the lot and into her Harvard boy's arms—glances moved away as quickly as they came. But I softened, looking on longingly at her spritely excitement; sure, I was an independent woman, but I was also a twenty-year-old girl. He looked nice enough across the way—kind eyes, big smile—

Beer splashed across my shirt.

"Shit! I'm so sorry!" Someone profusely apologized.

I didn't glance up, as my face flushed at the sound of roaring, obnoxious jeers.

"Take your shirt off, sweetheart!" cried a drunken creep.

"Yeah, free the nipple!" another spewed.

"Mind your fucking manners, boys!" the culprit barked back.

I peered up at him—his empty solo cup in hand—ready to unleash a heated tirade—

"Again, I'm so sorry. Let me just—" he took off his Harvard sweatshirt, handing it out to me without a thought. "I mean you've got a century-long streak over us—" he gestured to my shirt, his crooked grin growing with a boyish charm I'd come to love. "But it's all I got."

I took a beat, as I filled with an insurmountable urge to just—laugh. He made me laugh.

His blue eyes sparkled with relief and something else—

"I'm Wesbrooke." He leaned in for a hug—that my frigid upbringing did not prepare me for. But if anyone could melt an ice queen ... "No worries—I splashed us past that awkward stage."

And from there, it was the-never-ending day. After a few beers and meaningless-meaningful conversations, we combined our groups. First, we headed to Harpoon Brewery—more beer, as I shared my thoughts on the *Feminist Mystique*, while poor Wes politely feigned interest; then a rock show at the Paradise Club—even more beer, Wes made a friend ... friend brought us backstage ... friend took off his sunglasses ... friend was Jon Bon Jovi. Last, we headed to Wes's fraternity—the legendary Harvard Porcellian Club—for an after-party. Stacey and I wobbled along, arm-in-arm, laughing at this night's shenanigans: we were about to walk into an exclusive Harvard frat, after catching an icon wandering through (excuse my French) a shitty Boston night club. We didn't have the Snapchat back then, so naturally, we thought—

"No one is gonna believe us, Bizzy Lizzy," Stacey cackled, as Wes held the front door for us.

"After you, Bizz," Wes grinned.

"Excuse me, kind sir," Stacey impudently corrected, "ya' not quite there yet."

"Oh yeah? Well, tough crowd."

We passed through a hallway of ancient portraits.

"How 'bout Bitsy? See, I made it my own!"

"Good luck, lover boy!" Stacey hollered as she continued down the hall with her date.

Before we could join them on the Porcellian grand tour, Wes's eyes stared back at me from a different era.

"Oh, that's just the old man." Wes put his arm around me as I eyed a portrait hanging along the wall. "He was sure a character in his day."

I then looked down at a long, obnoxious name engraved on a gold plate: Wesbrooke Dodge Ellison VII.

"A mouthful, huh?"

"Not if you go by *Wes*." I smirked.

•

Then came the moment of truth, as guests filtered out, Stacey disappeared, and I sat kissing Wes on Porcellian's parlor couch. Mother always said nothing good ever happens past midnight; although I preached women's sexual liberation to whomever cared to listen, all I could hear was that ticking grandfather clock in the corner, counting down my Christian guilt. I finally pulled away to glare at the old thing, but instead, I noticed a beautiful mahogany piano; it looked identical to the one from my childhood home. I excitedly ran over to the bench, mesmerized as I ran my fingers along the familiar, mahogany hexagonal engravings lining the cover—I wondered if Porcellian boys went to tag sales.

"An art curator, clothes designer, pianist ..." Wes sat beside me, "you're the whole package."

I smiled shyly,

"When I was a little girl, Wes, I had a piano *just* like this. I never took lessons though. I played by ear. But honestly," I lightly laughed to myself. "I just wanted to learn 'Close to You' by The Carpenters. It was my favorite growing up."

"Well, let's hear it!"

I confidently positioned my hands along the keys; they had a mind and memory of their own. And no matter how much time would pass, I would always come back and—

"Wait, let me just—" I tried again.

Then again … and again—my cacophonous, failed attempts drowning out the ticking clock beside us.

As tears suddenly brimmed my eyes, Wes gently stopped me, taking my hand in his.

"Hey," he said softly.

I stared down at my feet.

"It's a good thing you can't play—hold tight." He stole a kiss on my cheek before swooping over to the parlor's record player. He quickly swiped through their collection, happily humming to himself. Meanwhile, I brushed away those pesky tears, praying my mascara hadn't ran.

"Ah ha!" He found the album, placing it on the turntable.

"A Carpenters album in a frat house?" I lightly giggled. "Quite the enigma."

"First and foremost, we are not a *frat*, we are a *final club*. Very different—a worldly, sensitive bunch, you see."

I rolled my eyes.

"So, I'll pardon your faux pas, just this once, if … and only if …"

He put his hand out for a dance.

As we swayed together, I fit comfortably in the crook of his neck, surprised by my own vulnerability.

"I want to take you on a date," I declared, redeeming my feminist stronghold, "Stacey has a play coming up. She's a real showstopper."

"I don't know, Bitsy—might make you work for it." He retorted in mock exasperation … with that haunting crooked grin.

Our Brookes was a ham in his early childhood years. I remember picking him up one day; he was performing what I perceived as a one man show for his classmates. All the kids sat gathered around a wooden mini jungle gym with a tiny cabin underneath. They giggled, shoving one another for a better seat. Suddenly, Brookes popped out from the cabin. He was dressed to the nines with a crown, purple cape, and detachable lion tail—all brought together with his cheeky stage presence. It was fascinating to watch my son in action. He stood at the top of the jungle gym, narrating his made-up tales like an old wise man storyteller from a Disney movie. As he went along, he held up intricate watercolor paintings of animals and nature. They were rather good for his age. I was amazed; he was like a mini, male Beatrix Potter, the way he brought things to life through story and art. His teacher, Mrs. Corrigan, called Wes and me in for a meeting the next day.

"Your son has a gentle heart and a wild imagination," laughed Mrs. Corrigan. "I truly encourage him to pursue art."

I excitedly called up Stacey. She was now an established actress, and helped me schedule an exclusive beginners acting course that Friday. Wes took him out on a hunting trip instead.

You know, we drove here together—just Wes and I. This wasn't what I wanted, but it felt appropriate. It didn't feel right; it felt appropriate. We drove in silence, both of our minds elsewhere, anywhere from the horror of the present. Instead, I focused on another horror—our marriage. You would think this would make matters worse; perhaps I'd pop pills, hang a noose, jump—drown myself, just as Wes had drowned our life savings. But believe it or not, counteracting pain can bring you to this inexplicable level of inertia. You continue on with your daily life, looking down at your stagnant, clandestinely broken self; and while you function on the surface, you're dead underneath the seams of normalcy. I did try to sew my life back together. I remarried, I moved, I started yoga. Brookes was away at boarding school, so I didn't have to worry about him.

As we drove along, we passed our home. I noticed a young Hispanic woman at the end of our neighbor's driveway. She walked hand-in-hand with a little boy, no more than four years old, towards the house. He had a fire engine red backpack that he struggled with as he hobbled along. She endearingly scooped the child, kissing his fat, little cheeks as if he were her own. Suddenly, my breath grew quick and my vision blurred. Wes pulled over as I began violently dry heaving—gulping for air in the seemingly oxygen-less space around me. Before I knew it, I was on his lap blacking in and out of consciousness. He held me close. He said nothing. This didn't feel appropriate. It felt right.

As mourners enter the church, I grasp Joel's hand to my right; it's gentle and reassuring—it's safe. Wes lightly pulls at my other but I stare stoically ahead. I can feel the prying eyes of family, friends, and acquaintances behind us. I want to reject his gesture but they're watching, waiting—gathering. My hand is squeezed in a tight fist, fingernails digging dangerously deep, anger building—*buzzzzzzzzzzzz*. My eyes dart around in frantic, vexing frustration. Who leaves a goddamn window open at a—Wes unclenches my fist. I glance at him and my anger disintegrates. He and Brookes have an almost identical profile. Brookes had my eyes, but his bone structure was all Wes. Wes is Brookes. We are Brookes. We created and destroyed this child together.

Then, I see it—just sitting there on my baby's portrait. The bee—the source of that incessant, unrelenting, buzzing. It's just sitting there. No one's acknowledging it. No one's saying anything. But I know they see it. They know it's there, but they're not doing anything. As it crawls across my son's face, slow and steady, making a mockery of its path, I notice its color ... it's shape ... it's shell. It's not a bee—it's a wasp. *Buzzzzzzzzzzzzzzzz*.

I jolt out of my seat.

"SHUT UP! JUST SHUT UP!"

PART II:

GOD SAKE THE KING

I could stand at the podium and say that Wesbrooke—ninth of our name—was my buddy—my little old sport. I'd pause, look to everyone in the room—look *through* everyone in the room—and smile within the comfort of complacent comedic relief. I'd grin like a jester without a bell-rimmed hat, as I tap my feet to the too-regulated beat of my heart. But no one—not one single person—will clap to this quiet plea. Maybe I'll even throw in a light laugh—keep it safe and self-aware. I could stand at the podium and say that my namesake, junior—or *joon-ya*, we'd joke. Alright, a Sopranos quip at a funeral—at your son's funeral, you idiot? I could stand at the podium and ... and ... I could stand at the podium and break.

Right now, I'm a role—that's all they want me to be. I'm nothing but a puppet figurehead of a title, and I wish I didn't play the part so damn well. As I stare blankly ahead, I realize I'm not a person—this has depleted me of all humanity—so I'm just a role. The father, the patriarch—the godforsaken king, if you will. God sake the King ... please, God—Jesus, Buddha, Mohammad, whatever's out there—sake the King. I look in my peripherals at Prime Minister Jackass Joel seated next to our Queen. He fulfills his duties on autopilot when I cannot—a dedicated discount leader through and through.

But, from the get-go, I saw the wheels behind his cagey eyes turn at the sight of wealth and rising status. God has yet to save the Queen. But I didn't want to believe it, honest. I really wanted her to be happy. Nonetheless, Joel will never take the throne—I have the title. However, it's all anyone expects from me—all they want. Not our Elizabeth though, despite her uncanny detachment. So I look on at my ex-wife—longer than propriety allows—as I trace her ageless profile. I use every ounce of my strength not to kiss the parallel beauty marks resting on her temple—where my lips always fit perfectly in between. People think matching tattoos are bad, try laser removing your human puzzle piece.

Elizabeth sits with her back too straight, chest barely rising—has she even blinked? And I'll stare even longer if I don't get answers—if I don't see a speck of humanity within the miniscule moment it takes to shed a single tear. Our son is an empty body, but somehow, he's more present than this living corpse beside me. But I'll wait for her to wake—longer than the time it takes to identify a body at a morgue. They know me there, Bitsy. They'll give me six more hours this time. Because when I grasp your cold hand, I believe you'll squeeze back—

Her hand moves away as she whips her torso around—perhaps meeting an icy whisper with an even cooler glare.

"Bitz, are you alright?" I ask because I mean it—with all of my heart, Elizabeth.

She nods because she doesn't.

What a stupid fucking question.

I'm one body, one man. That's all I can be. I'm no superhero. A body, a man, a name ... but does a body make a man with a name?

Does a name make a man with a body? Bitsy's ninety-six-year-old aunt glares at me, probably pissed she stuck around to see the wrong Wesbrooke kick it—a man makes a body with a name—too senile to speak, too evil to relent those beady, squawking vulture eyes— dammit, I can't even look. Oh, you didn't know eyes could talk? Well, they don't ... they scream. Look close enough and listen as she *squawks* and waits, *squawks* and waits, *squawks* and waits, for a father, an ex-husband, and a nuisance to break. Not a Lost Boy, Brooksie. That's all you were. And everyone knew it. So, rest easy little old sport—your sacred body's safe with me. I won't let her peck. How 'bout that for this goddamn podium. So I sit upright, head forward, back strong—I won't let *them* peck. It's me they want, son, but don't worry—us Lost Boys live forever.

The Green Vale School, Brookes's old grade school, puts on a play every spring: *Peter Pan*. Brookes could sing, he could dance— but, most important, that kid could make you laugh. He was far too young and small to fit the title role but we were sure he had it in the bag. Bitz and I sat for a glass of wine or two as we enjoyed our little one man show. We watched as he bounced around the living room, playing out his audition scene in ten different ways, over and over to the point where we had Peter Pan right at our dinner table. Now, that's what I call method acting. Green Vale called it a supporting role—so they made him a Lost Boy. I want to say he was the best damn Lost Boy on that stage, but I'd be lying. He took his heart out of it, transforming fervor to hate and frustration—as if the entire world owed him their undying love and attention. Some call it passion, others—well—only child syndrome. Junior was either all in or all out. I figured he needed to channel this boyish rage somewhere, so I snuck us off to a father-son hunting trip that weekend. Prepared with matching coon hats and camouflage, we played around like the real Lost Boys we were.

Hey, shoot me. There's no book on how to be a parent; we raise them the best we can, from what we know, and hope they don't grow up to be sociopaths—or libertarians. So, I raised my son in my family estate, just as father did … and his father … and so forth. Yes, we're *that* American family; our bloodline ran as deep as our legacy of dysfunction.

Now, I bet you're picturing my old man in his day—some rich, handsomely brutish, womanizing Long Island douchebag, jumping his polo pony right out of the pages of *The Great Gatsby*. From his stunning Harvard Porcellian Club portrait, to the *New York Times*'s "Most Eligible Bachelor" cotillion coverage. He looked the part— that's for damn sure—then he'd open his mouth.

Let's take a trip down Porcellian's legacy lane. You'll find generations of Ellison men, lining a wall of inductee portraits, as old as the college itself. Keep walking down that hall and transport decades back to a common room, filled with Harvard's finest scholars. They score expertly through their studies, ready to be this country's next-best-whatever. However, their eyes dart up to an abrupt disruption in the center of the room—who would even dare? Well, that lofty theater fella' sure would, as his attractively punchable face twists and contorts to a melodramatic audition monologue.

"Hey, whaddaya say?" one hollers in annoyance. "Go practice somewhere else!"

"Real class act, Ellison, real class act!" another chimes in, chucking a crumpled piece of notebook paper at the guy.

"Harvard man to starving artist. Just what that legacy of yours needs—"

"And a partridge in a pear tree!" someone sing-songs, as the entire room erupts with laughter.

So, how does such a man—with the impunity of enough privilege to own his choice of countenance—retaliate? The only way he knows, as he angrily holds up a shaking fist.

"Why, I oughta—" *Boom*—and he's royally knocked out.

Suffice to say, Grandpa never got the lead either, Brooksie.

Then flip through that December '65 *Times* issue, and admire the dazzling debutante, posed arm in arm with a beaming, slick haired aristocratic stud. If they had iPhone "live" back then, this picture would tell a thousand words. You'd hold your finger on the screen, as Father suavely licks his palm, smoothing over his pompadour like a cheeky Looney Tune; his date's big, beautiful smile diminishes in disgust. Nonetheless, she sees past this titillating sophistication and into a future of financial security and a solid blue-blooded lineage; Father was the original "catfish."

As this heiress threw her pole, he swam further into his own head. So much so, that he broke off their engagement, dropped out of Harvard, and chased his dreams—as well as an up-and-coming model—to Hollywood and back. Literally—he was back in two months. The reality of drama beyond a theater stage was romantic in theory, horrifying in practice. He didn't have that "star factor," as Joel would've keyed. Still, Hollywood big-wigs called him into their offices out of sheer curiosity and patronizing amusement—they sure knew who Wesbrooke Dodge Ellison was. Because he wasn't a Coppola, a Ford or a Meyer; he was—

"just a pretentious trust-bust-dodging capitalist pig living off of child-labor-mogul-money!"—his ambitious model-turned-pregnant-hippie reminded him, to her own misfortune.

This was a parallel universe, where liberal jurisdiction and nouveau riche validation mattered, and it threw Father into a debilitating backwards loop. So he spiraled back to the North Shore of Long Island with the wave of an Irish farewell and a lofty child support check; this was as laissez-faire as the man would get. Now, all was right in his world, as he reengaged the heiress, reenrolled into Harvard, and reassimilated into high society as quickly as he had left it.

However, Father came home more popular than he bargained for. His Hollywood stint was not seen as a failure but as an enigma; people were all ears at Piping Rock dinners, living vicariously through each exaggerated adventure from the safety of their pretentious bubble. Meanwhile, his true life's drama was paid away without the slightest regard. But as his favorite playwright, Oscar Wilde, once said, "Life imitates art, far more than art imitates life." And soon enough, a letter arrived in the mail with my mother's death announcement.

I was only a year old when I arrived at Ellison Manor, respectfully, as … Garfunkel Rainman Connelly. May my mother's free-spirited soul rest in peace, but this was the dumbest, bohemian bullshit name in the baby book and I thank God every single day that I was born two decades earlier than the film you are presumably cackling about right now. However, to Father's fiancé's horror, I was renamed Wesbrooke Dodge Ellison VIII—a powerhouse lineage handed down to a bastard. But Father was a young, new dad with a healthy baby boy … and a guaranteed heir.

Father played "Wesbrooke" as if it were his tangible Oscar-nod. He'd observe his preppy peers, mismatching each semblance in hopes of piecing together his own. But, his phony smile and inconsistent countenance appeared manic and, frankly, desperate; folks tired over the same Hollywood tales told a trillion different, excitable ways. Yet there *I* was, the last remnant of his peak years—well, months—and he hauled me around like a tragic circus animal. People looked on at me, shy and detached, with pity rather than interest; they certainly thought I was special, just not in the way my deplorable father had hoped. However, he managed to find a fellow underdog friend in our neighbor, Mr. Compton.

Every day, Father waited for my school bus at the corner of Valley and Crescent. North Country Colony's road was too long and narrow for a giant school bus, yet too dark and isolated for a seven year-old to make the trek home alone. The whole neighborhood consisted of a mile-long, gated loop of old Gold Coast homes located in the city of Glen Cove. I'd hop off the bus, smiling with glee, knowing damn well I could've been tossed off to a pack of nannies for any matters of care and general human decency. Each time, my tiny hand held securely in his, I'd observe him peacefully eyeing the surrounding wood.

"Father, I'm cold." I shivered in my Green Vale blazer against the chilly mid-fall air.

"Well, that's tough, little old sport," he responded, selfishly cozying up to his rabbit-fur-lined Brooks Brothers fleece.

I smiled sweetly with anticipation, catching the start of our one and only inside joke.

"What's tough?" I asked excitedly.

"Life," he responded in mock-disappointment, rehashing his bad acting days.

"What's *Life*?"

"A magazine."

"Where'd ya get it?"

"The five-and-dime."

"How much?"

"A dime. How much ya got?"

"A nickel." I said with a sigh as Father laughed.

To give you some context, Americans concocted this little charade during the Great Depression. It's not like the Ellison clan went through it or anything—they hid their money under mattresses and dodged trust-busters like the plague—but it was fun to pretend.

"That's tough," Father concluded.

"What's tough?"

This could go on forever—

"Life."

—and I always hoped it would.

"What's *Life*?"

We reached the Woolworth estate and father got quiet. He looked on curiously at this abandoned, crumbling spectacle of a lost time, formerly owned by F. W. Woolworth of the Woolworth five-and-dime stores (think CVS Pharmacy of the 1920s). Upon the 1929 crash, his empire was the first to plummet, yet his home has been one of the last grand mansions standing; most have ended up bulldozed or transformed into decadent catering halls. I looked up and caught Father's eyes dilating in an unearthly dead gaze—perhaps, an involuntary physiological response of admiration and or pure fear. I still don't know which. But both walked hand in hand with us down that narrow path.

Every day, Mr. Compton sat on his rickety front stoop, slumped on a rocking chair with a glare as bitter as the brandy sloshing around his glass. As we'd walk by, I'd catch a frazzled Mrs. Compton, squirreling around their perpetually unkempt property. She'd neurotically whack, weed, and avoid Mr. Compton's commands as if her sanity depended on it. So I'd hobble a little faster, hoping Father would follow my lead. Then, like clockwork—

"May! Rake the leaves!"

"May! Clean the sheets!"

"May! Cut the meat!"

"May! Another drink!"

And each time, Father whipped around enthusiastically, as if his only friend hollered a how-do-you-do.

"Well, how do you do, Mr. Compton?"

"I've seen better days, Wesy-boy, I've seen better days," Mr. Compton slurred.

I heaved a sigh of defeat as Father disappointedly dropped my hand and swung the door to their rotted fence.

"What happened, bud?" Father inquired.

"Another good man down." Mr. Compton proclaimed, pointing to a shadow of a Rottweiler standing behind their first-floor window curtain.

No, this was not the silhouette of a ghost dog …

"Again?! Say, what's May feeding those poor suckers?"

"May! Stop killing the damn dog!" Mr. Compton screamed to his own amusement, as his wife responded with a violent tug at a flowerbed.

I nervously peered up at their second floor window, knowing all too well what glowered down at me through—

"Yeah, come on," Father cheekily added. "We need 'em for our trips!"

—glassy, inanimate, taxidermy eyes.

"Say it louder, my boy!" Mr. Compton added. "Our good Lord's got another angel, my wife's got another security guard. You never know what's lurking in these woods nowadays, what with all the Italians sullying up the township."

Back then, Glen Cove was half WASP, half everyone else. There's no other way to put it. However, I find it funny that during the town's Gold Coast heyday, elite families planted their extravagant homes upon acres and acres of Indian burial ground. Now, at this point, the majority of the town consisted of cheap subdivisions built upon broken, post-recession dreams. However, North Country Colony was (and still is) nothing short of an elite compound, keeping reality at bay beyond its steel gates.

"Well, when Glen Cove gives you lemons, make Limoncello, ol' boy!" Father said in cheeky anticipation, as if he had this joke saved in his back pocket for weeks—which he probably did.

Mr. Compton howled with laughter as he leaned back in his chair—dangerously close to its tipping point.

"Hey, didn't you have the little one with you?" He inquired as he wiped away tears.

By then, I had bolted off.

Right now, sitting directly before my son's lifeless body, I want to laugh—a growing cackle of insanity like Heath Ledger's Joker, or the actor himself. I want the world to see what—not who—I am. Or what we all are, rather. Because no matter how many pills we pop to mask our pain, *we are* the empty jar. Then I'll die—two men in one Lost Boy. They'll see my performance, then I'll be free. Or I'll try living for something—not somebody—for once. When your heart breaks like this, you discover that every precious life's a silent killer. As I reach for Bitsy's hand, she pulls away, hitting the last note on this *Lost Boy Swan Song.* She quickly twitches to turn around, as if she hears my audience's cheers. I want to rise and bow.

Laughing and crying are one and the same, they say. I quote that from Bitsy's college reunion dinner party years back. I returned from work that night, quietly tip-toeing past the hens in my living room. As I reached the safe-haven of our kitchen, I filled up a plate of food, just ready to sneak off when—

"Oh hey, honey!" Bitsy suddenly announced, loud and proud for her ladies to hear, casually leaning against the doorway into the living room like a freakin' Jedi. She stuck her tongue out at me with a cheeky, teasing grin—all airs for our stuck-up friends, but a goofball at heart. I slit my hand across my throat, fantasizing about sparing myself the torture. Plus, the little guy and I had steady plans to watch Tim Burton's *Batman* before bed—shit, was he too small for that one?

The night was young and I, too sober, as Bitsy's silver-spooned Emerson girlfriends fed each other's intellectually enlightened egos at my dinner table. I caught her friend Susan Brockton, eyeing me down, as if I were sexier than the piece of prime rib sitting on my tragically untouched plate.

"Well, look who decided to show up!" She drunkenly leered, sporting the empty confidence of an unattractive floozy feminist.

You can loosen that tight bun, Sue, we've all witnessed your wild prime.

"Let's get your take, Wes," she continued. "You have two heightened extremes: a laugh and a cry."

"A laugh, a cry—one and the same, I say!" exclaimed God-knows-who.

Sue absentmindedly swirled her wine glass in thought, scarlet nectar coiling in dangerous rotation near the rim. I caught Bitsy's nervous eye, darting from Susan's unsteady hand to her favorite carpet.

Fucking Sue, just drink the damn thing before you give my wife a heart attack.

"Should we, as a society, determine the propriety of one over the other? They warrant the same emotional response."

This random concept jumped out at me … I took a beat.

"Certainly not. But I have one question for you—"

The hens clucked me off—apparently, I misjudged the complexity within these extreme emotional responses. Yet, I didn't even respond.

I rolled my eyes with a dramatic huff. You can't win with these people. Naturally, this called for a warning head whack from Bitz before she leaned across the table to collect plates. In turn, she got a swift slap on the ass.

The hens pecked.

"Keep your hands to yourself!" one clucked.

"Hyper-masculinity at its finest," one scoffed.

And things like that.

Bitz shook her head disapprovingly before I caught a quick, cute, smirk—gave her away every time.

I didn't pry, but I sympathized with these women—this was definitely the most action they had witnessed in ten years. So I did their hot-and-bothered consciences a favor and reeled us back to the subject at hand.

"As I was saying, my smart Alice's, I have one question. Would any of you laugh at a funeral?"

"MUA HA HA HA, DADDY!" seven-year-old Brookes abruptly hollered, lurking by the door frame with Blankey draped across his face like a stealth movie villain. Susan popped up with a start, finally splashing that glass of red. I don't know what scared the existential profundity out of that woman more: Brookes's abrupt entrance or that filthy, ratted, moth-snack he carried everywhere.

Bitsy's favorite, functioning alcoholics shifted in their chairs, chirping in forcibly polite unison over the innocent interruption.

This riled us up even more.

"Together now, Junior! Give these old broads a show!"

I promise you, Susan stopped everything to glance at her reflection in a tablespoon.

"MUA HA HA HAAAA!" We hollered together in defiance as I jumped out of my chair, scooping up my doppelganger troublemaker-in-arms.

"Wesbrooke!" Bitsy barked too sharply, making Susan jolt again in her chair—and splatter more red. "Get over here. Right now. And apologize to Mrs. Brockton."

"Which one?" I asked in mock-innocence.

The hens chuckled now. Elizabeth did not.

Little Wesbrooke clung to me for dear life, freezing in place like a shaken baby doe.

Come on, Bitz, lower your voice—you know better than that. Next time, just spend a little under 10k for a rug.

Instead, I whispered gently to Brookes, coaxing him into a comfortable calm as I slowly walked us over to Susan. As I lowered us down to her seated level, we expressed our—

"Apologies, Mrs. Brockton." We recited in perfect harmony.

Brookes quickly leaned in, planted a soft kiss on her cheek and reverted to the safe crook of my neck. *That should do it.*

"We come and leave in peace, ladies." I said, E. T. hand gesture and all.

I twirled Brookes in my arms, up and out of the hen den, with one last "mua ha, haaa" of reassurance in his ear.

When we reached the outer corridor, I flipped him over, about to fake catapult him into the air as he shifted himself into a Superman pose.

"You ready yet, buddy?" I asked.

Brookes pushed his right arm forward, eyes dead set to fly down the long, narrow path ahead.

"I'm ready, Daddy."

But I was not.

"Let's make a deal. Play today, fly tomorrow?"

His little body went limp in disappointment—dramatic whimper and all. I pulled him back up to face me.

"Come on, little old sport. Batmans-in-training don't—"

He rubbed tears away under his new round-rimmed, high optical glasses. Bitsy thought he looked like Harry Potter—as if she knew even an inkling about men's fashion. But they were not glasses anymore, they were microscopes. Have you ever looked in a mirror and not recognized yourself? You look so hard at your reflection that it's no longer your own. Your heart skips a beat, in this millisecond of fear, as you become all too self-aware of an impending stranger. Now, look into the eyes of your firstborn child.

"Daddy—are you *wreally* the *wreal* Batman?"

"As real as he gets, Brooksie."

"But are you *cewreal*?"

"I'm super cereal," I responded in my best Batman voice. "With ten extra grams of protein!"

Brookes giggled.

"Strong, fearless … invisible!" Brookes proclaimed with pride.

He might as well have cursed me out. In fact, I would rather he had.

"Indivisible," I reluctantly corrected.

"Indi—indiva," He stuttered, struggling to articulate.

I abruptly placed him down. Dark spots clouded my vision as I felt for the cold, antique knob to my home office, feigning casualty against my skyrocketing heart rate. As I fumbled with the old thing, I caught oblivious Brookes matching his little feet in between the designs on the hallway carpet. This simple act brought me to a place of momentary calm. He was clueless, as he patiently jumped between the intricate patterns, just waiting to be scooped up and acknowledged again. I stared down this pod of a patriarch in horror, genuinely forgetting where and who I am. But Brookes never did; time doesn't stop for your children. They catch a glimpse of your madness and never forgive you—or they become you.

Brookes absent-mindedly looked up. "Can I come in the Batcave too, Daddy? Just this once?"

I squirreled into the room, shutting the heavy mahogany door behind me. As he pounded at the door, I leaned against it in shame. But each tiny thump of frustration felt like a light tap on the back—a friendly reminder of my worth. Sometimes your heart beats so loud that you keep your back turned when the soul comes knocking. But one day—and I promise you this day will come—you'll turn around. And when you do, don't be strong; fall into the abyss of mania. Feel something before it's too late.

Suddenly, a loud, hearty thump woke me from my reverie, practically catapulting me off the door. Brookes's cries sounded clean and clear now, immediately throwing me out of my internal detriment. I jumped back into the present, rewinding myself into sanity as I swung the door opened. Brookes clutched Bitsy's thigh like a lifeline as her red, bruised hand stroked his shoulder. As I leaned down to quell him, he moved behind her, eyes suspicious and fearful—unforgiving.

"Brookes, go watch a movie," she demanded in a steady monotone.

He wouldn't move.

"What did I say?" she repeated, a little harsher.

My mouth hung open, but my words rang solely in my head.

No, he needs us right now, Bitsy.

Brookes ran off in tears as Elizabeth calmly glided into the room, heavy door closing lightly behind her as if she double-teamed with the ghosts of this ancient manor.

In one habitual swoop, she leaned into my desk drawer and pulled out a pill bottle. She underhanded it to me, making the save before our rival team hit home base. Be careful, when your wife plays ball with your demons, she might actually win.

My hand shook as I looked down uncertainly at the thing.

"So, are you gonna take one or be a manic mess for the rest of the night?" she questioned degradingly, hand on her waist as if I were the problem child of the household. "I'll wait."

"But Brookes—"

"He'll be fine—"

Tears filled my weary eyes.

"Unless *you* aren't."

Twenty minutes later I was Batman again.

Ironically enough, my extremes were what Bitsy loved the most. She used to call it passion. Now she calls it petulance. She was an aspiring artist; I was a training stockbroker. But opposites attract after one too many at a Harvard tailgate. We were drunk, she was the cutest thing I ever did see, and that's how babies are made, Brooksie. Oh calm down, he'd get a kick out of that one—I'd get a shove and an "eww," but boy, did that little old sport like a good, crude joke.

She talked and talked, like most girls do, but this time I listened. Her beautiful lips wrapped around each syllable as if everything she said were an urgent tall tale that needed to be told. And she had this calming, musical voice—like a children's librarian—that made you want to hone in or take a peaceful nap. When I told her this, she scrunched her cute nose and laughed, thanking me for such a strange compliment. She'd never met someone so genuine. I blushed because I wasn't. I laughed because I was.

I'd like to think that's why we drove here together—just she and I. I wanted to believe that there was something left—

I read to her under a tall oak in the Harvard Yard, her delicate body nestled onto my lap against the brisk New England breeze.

"The believer will open his mind to the truth on condition that it fits in with his preconceived ideas and wishes. Faith, on the other hand, is an unreserved opening of the mind to the truth, whatever it may turn out to be. Faith has no preconceptions; it is a plunge into the unknown. Belief clings, but faith lets go." I recited Alan Watts, a popular, debatably zany, Zen philosopher, from his novel *The Wisdom of Insecurity.*

"I like that," she said. "There's so much that we don't understand—that we'll never quite understand."

"I think he's a kook. Can't believe my professor's having us read this liberal garbage."

"Well I have *faith* that you'll get through it."

She smirked up at me, leaning in for a kiss, but I was lost in thought as I looked out at my peers. Their noses sat shoved in books, suffocating their souls with the knowledge endowed by America's first and finest collegiate institution.

"I believe we all will. Whatever *it* is. But they'll never let us go."

—I *had* to believe that there was something left. I needed a notion of love—a memory, a motive, an objective torn from this long-alienated emotion. I've bled faith into it until I've had to understand my role; a man can't be a lover and a provider. I failed you, Bitz. Not just you—I failed an establishment. Junior followed, but at the end of the day, he conquered, as he lies peacefully ahead of us. Those damn schools were just a name—a name makes a man without a body— and he was just a boy. I wanted him to stay—I needed to sculpt him from the unknown I created—that I tried too late to amend. Why do you think we called him Brookes? They believed in Wesbrooke—along with eight previous generations—but we had faith in Brookes. So I sat there in that car until you stopped believing in me. And I'll continue to hold you close in my arms until faith eventually sets us both free.

I watch Joel grasp Bitsy's hand as her chest heaves a sigh of relief—not love, relief. I reach for her other because I know what she needs—what we both need—before this funeral commences. But her hand sits tightly clenched on her lap, soft lips pursed, veins pulsating against her beauty-marked temple, all in the name of emotional restraint until—she turns around once more to Brookes's mourners. I've had it. I grab her hand securely in mine. Her body's ready for war but her eyes, held directly on me now, are a white flag waving with the purity and beauty of surrender. And in her vulnerability I saw her again—I saw Brookes again. She turns forward, eyes widening in awe for what lies ahead, as I swiftly kiss her temple—my temple … our faith.

PART III:

TO QUELL THE PIOUS ATHEIST

I could stand at the podium and say that Wesbrooke—that young man and his long, uppity name—was a show-stopping presence in our household. I'd feel awkward in my wording, dismiss Wes's eye roll, and ramble on confidently in my ability to appease these silent hecklers. Everyone's a critic. I could stand at the podium and say that my stepson—the child I never wanted but am glad I had—was a congenial wise guy. Throw 'em with a quirky oxymoron to lighten the mood; they'll need it after Wes's predictably pathetic preceding speech. I could stand at the podium and say that from the moment I met the kid, I knew a star was a born—Ventura Agency's Joel Fuchs for crying out loud, it's my job to spot these things! Then I could stand and wait for Wes to knock that podium right over and me with it. I guess I shouldn't say any of this—not a goddamn thing.

That hot shot, Plato, once said, "Wise men speak because they have something to say; fools because they have to say something." I learned this when I married into Elizabeth's family—wait a minute, shouldn't it be the other way around? She *is* Elizabeth Fuchs now, after all. Marrying late in life, without your own seeds sown so to speak, can be funny like that. You're already an outlier to family dynamics the minute you set foot into their sphere. Meanwhile, I plunged nine generations deep into a patriarchal pit of American aristocracy. And when you walk against the grain, you're heard like a lion rustling in the dried reeds of a barren field searching for water; suddenly, those beautiful, thirst-struck gazelles spot you. They're all worked up, ready to run before you're even a threat. Your presence unnerves them, but you, too, are just looking for a drink in this desolate land. There are predators, there are prey, and the pursuit of a stiff cold one—Jesus, I should just start my own religion. Because I had a voice and I used it—whether people wanted to hear it or not. And that's what Elizabeth loved the most about me. I didn't succumb to her one-dimensional world's prejudiced preconceptions nor heed her husband's petty precautions. I'd say my peace, and if they didn't like it, that was their problem—never mine. But sitting here today, staring ahead at my albatross, it's as if I didn't say a word.

Sometimes I wish I could step right out—be nonexistent to the chaos I unwittingly brought onto my—Wes's—family. After what I did, they will always be his. But he doesn't know that as he wallows in his empty guilt. No one does and ever will. I close my eyes and I see it—the plastic baggie, the substance. I involuntarily shake my head out of the memory, forgetting where I am for a moment. I'm sitting in the front row at my stepson's funeral—that's where I am— for the audience to observe the mourning relatives. My face flushes; there's something so violating about getting lost in your head. You've checked out of the real world and into the deep subconscious realm of the mind, subjected to literature and art films. In other words, people on the outside think you look like a fucking weirdo. But you'd think I'd be safe at a time like this; people overlook the quirks of the grieving, right? No, they don't. They wonder why the mother isn't crying—perhaps she never loved her child; they judge the ex-husband for being quiet—he's always been such a snob; and most horrifyingly, they'll question the new spouse—what's he trying to forget?

Maybe, if I sit still enough in this seat, I'll just disappear. The emptiness reverberating throughout my existence will manifest itself from soul to body. It'll be grander than any magic trick a person could muster. I'll be unforgettable *and* I'll be free—like Julia Roberts in *Sleeping with the Enemy*. Suddenly, Elizabeth whips her head around to eye the crowd behind us. She's probably checking on that decrepit aunt of hers; thank God that old bitty likes me because she hates—I reel back in disgust as the air settles within the *whish* of Elizabeth's long, blonde locks. She smells like cologne. Not just any cologne: Wes's goddamn over-priced musky muck. There's nothing good about a funeral besides the calming smell of goddamn flowers, and here I am, choking over this man's stench flowing from my wife's hair.

I can't smell the roses, but I can admire Brookes's portraits sitting upon his closed casket like a reverse drama mask placed over a stage. His smile is the same, but those eyes—they give us away every time. There's truly nothin' like a trusting smile. It takes effort but we do it everyday; we push one out for the kids. The job. The spouse. A smile is everything and nothing. It's safe within its beauty—it's art. It's not *an* art. It *is* art. We paint a portrait of assurance just far enough to quell a baby; land the job; beguile the lover. And our patrons will forever peruse the gallery, interpreting, critiquing … waiting in vain for originality within a world of archetypal brilliance. I can just see old Wesbrooke now, painting that generational smile, like a modern-day Picasso. He splatters a charmingly goofy grin, awaiting the climax of his own joke. However, he's sure to shade the chin, ever so slightly upward, to confirm that aristocratic countenance. The patron wants to believe in this masterpiece; they want to be in on its secret jest. But something doesn't feel quite right. Suddenly, they sit back in wonderment at this beautiful legacy of subtle ingenuity, because, by George, they've got it: they've been staring at a gold-plated title this entire time. Brookes is the joke, Wesbrooke is the punch line. Oh, that smile—boy, is it stunning in its superficiality, blinding the seer into creative compliance. There's truly nothing more dangerous than the deceased dilettante. Now the eyes—you catch every pain, sorrow, fear ... psychosis—

Cue the Oscar winner. I worked with these kinds of tortured souls every day at my agency, with their hearts screaming through sunken, worldly sockets, and talent brimming beneath broken-in smiles. You know you have something, when they walk into your office, and their smile doesn't match their eyes. Then you sit back, observe your subject, and sculpt madness into money. I was like Hollywood's Dr. Frankenstein; I'd mismatch emotions to create a raw, real piece of art: the malleable human. But Brookes—he already had that spark of electric personality; no one had to jolt him awake with metal rods of manipulative motivation. He was a star shining with his own light; this both repelled and fascinated me. Yet, he reeled me in to shut me out.

He was always sweet, docile little Brookes, ready to bother me in my office about anything and everything under the rainbow, from a book inquiry to the meaning of life. Wes never allowed him in the "Batcave," as Brookes called it. So, naturally, I was going to. I'm the first person to profess my disdain for younguns, but this one was different; Brookes would leave that office learning something new every day—and so did I. I can't even say that about most adults— let alone half of the dimwits I work with. There's really something special about speaking to a smart child; you get this eloquently articulated, PG-rated worldview.

"You're lucky kid," I concluded, taking a puff of a cigar as Brookes and I sat facing each other in my office's brown leather chairs. "You've got, not one, but two dads now." Elizabeth and I had just gotten married. Or tied the knot? Got officiated? It was a court wedding—give me a break.

Brookes placed his new square glasses on for distance as he peered out the window to his—our—Hundred-Acre Wood yard in thought.

I took a beat to admire those classy, new optics that I had just bought him—the sophisticated little stud! Now *there's* America's future.

"I guess so, but I don't really see my *real* dad much anymore."

I made Elizabeth reevaluate Wes's visitation rights. I wouldn't let his craziness rub off on our little guy here.

"Well, I don't see my real dad *at all* anymore," I added. "He died when I was fifteen."

Brookes gasped. I guess I never shared this before—and I still didn't want to, as I shifted awkwardly in my seat.

"Wow, that's so sad." He pushed his glasses up contemplatively. "I know you're old, but—"

"Easy there!" I jested, trying to keep my composure as light as day.

"Do you feel like you're fifteen when you think about him?"

Then I felt something in my chest—oh boy, definitely too much garlic at dinner. Heartburn is the worst.

I never answered the kid and he was intuitive enough not to ask again. But if I could do it all over, I would. As he grew into teenhood, I gradually lost him; I was within and without his world. Jesus, who am I—Nick-fucking-Carraway? I excelled in school but I never played sports; I loved art, as little Brookes once did, but what was all this paintball nonsense he was into? However, he never gave up on reading—something I pride myself on encouraging to this day. But that smart, budding Aristotle became a wise-ass yuppie practically the day I signed that goddam prep school tuition check. He was slowly but surely becoming Wesbrooke: not a man but a legacy. And he damn well knew it too. He replaced our secret-handshake high fives with polite yet dismissive nods in the hallway, bigoted—often anti-Semitic—jokes at dinner. Nonetheless, I desperately wanted to rekindle what we once had, and he was barely home for me to do it.

Come Thanksgiving break, I sat him down mano y mano—two men, two fat cigars. I really thought this would be exciting for him; he must feel like a caged animal over there. I went to sleepaway camp at fifteen, not boarding school. But Elizabeth persisted—I guess all the cool families were doing it. He puffed at that cigar like an expert, to my surprise, legs casually manspread as if he owned the goddamn place.

"Well, welcome back to my office!" I said with ironic cheer.

He glared at me in response as he took a giant puff, letting a long awkward silence lengthen the space between us.

"You mean my dad's office. I guess Mom got lucky in the

settlement—this place has been in my family for years." He looked around in simultaneous interest and disgust before scoffing in realization. "I guess technically that makes this my office. Welcome to *my* office, Papa Joel!"

He put his cigar out next to the astray on the side table, testing my patience with a knowing smirk.

You'd think I would've popped off; I'd order him to his room and ground him for the rest of his week of freedom. But, if I reacted, then he won. I wasn't his dad. I was his parent.

"Whiskey on the rocks with that stogie?" I cordially offered.

I solemnly nod to Elizabeth's great-aunt, playing my role as grief-stricken, strong-silent-type stepfather. She returns a tight smile, withholding eye contact to affirm my reluctantly welcomed countenance amidst her stainless lineage. But I'm here and I always will be. Bloodstains almost never come out. The color of apathy is so translucent; it's like that misty, ghoulish figure you just miss in the corner of your eye—those moments when you think you saw something and you probably did. Sweet, sweet apathy—you feel like the lead in your own shitty B-movie. You'll come across a few critics but essentially everyone falls for it and you're a box-office hit. Elizabeth certainly did—but if she swooshes her hair one more time, swaying Wes's unimaginable stench in my wake, I will surely give this audience something to talk about.

Rumors: you either run from them or run to them. You'll redirect curious small talk to the weather—*a hail storm in the middle of July, would ya think?* Redirect them to sports—*but how 'bout them Yankees?* On the flipside, you'll instigate a response from a floundering friend—*I'm only asking because I care.* Or my personal favorite—*I wasn't supposed to tell you, but* I am a closet shit-stirrer and made a career out of it. I had been running *to* nonsense so long, I started training for the New York City marathon for crying out loud. So I glided gracefully down the local hiking trail, my mind as impenetrable as the calluses beneath my feet. The path looped to create a pattern of yellowing leaves and a teasing view of the Long Island Sound just beyond. I pounded forward, fully aware of my strength and perseverance against the human extinct to slacken. This path won't change, it won't break—and neither would I—under any circumstances. However, I noticed something peculiar. After each loop, the view became clearer. Was I seeing things? It was seventy degrees in the middle of September; I presumed these leaves were holding on to this last hoorah of warmth as much as we all were. Nonetheless, each lap around proved me wrong and I chased the changing season.

After mile ten, I'd hit my limit, breathing heavily as I looked up at a now leafless view of the setting sun. The sun … son … stepson. Shit! I was supposed to meet Brookes at the bus stop and I was an hour late. However, today was his birthday and he was the big one-zero. I self-satisfyingly concluded that we are all inclined to instill some responsibility within this milestone. I never had a son, but I had always respectfully considered myself Brookes's surrogate father; a failed business venture just won't pay the bills, Wes. My sweet Elizabeth—cool and collected on the surface, yet her strength lay in not what she had conquered but in what she had endured all these years with that hung-up Harvard hotshot. The poor woman raised two boys; and it certainly showed, as I thought of her two new parallel frown lines. I named them Wes and Brookes, respectively. Now cue practical parent Papa Joel—the sitcom audience claps as he enters the stage with a confident wave. In most Jewish households, a boy becomes a man at thirteen; however, I resided in another man's former home—per "round-minded" Elizabeth's insistence—and I needed to get hold of things. So I dictated ten as the golden age of emotional deliverance. Brookes's walk home alone was the prime time to reflect and deflect upon prepubescent fears and attachments. And with this next step, we would be out of Ellison manor in no time—perhaps come spring? I had it all figured out.

In other words, I felt like I should be sweating over a ten mile run, not a ten-year-old who couldn't walk his damn self down a road. On the way back, I realized I was hightailing behind Wes's car, an obnoxiously fashionable, beat-up '95 Mercedes. We both turned into North Country Colony, our—my—private neighborhood, and my face drained as I spotted the inevitable up ahead. I watched the neighbor's bull-like Rottweilers gnawing and clawing at the dangerously rotted fence, matching the decrepit Victorian home beyond; their sharp teeth digging at the decaying flecks of wood as tiny Brookes sat shaking, terrified, on the grass directly in front of them. He rocked back and forth, cradling his sunburned little body to the rhythm of his own scream-cries. His hands quickly rose up to his ears, muffling them against the world and himself.

I easily could've driven on, sped past Wes's car as he pulled to the side of that narrow road. He'd dramatically leave his car door swung open for one of those wild neighborhood brats to ram right into. I'd feign blissful ignorance as I rushed home to Elizabeth to help prepare

Brookes's birthday dinner. When they returned, I'd play dumb; I'd even offer to pay for Wes's broken door. Wes would decline out of pride, shaking his head at the table as I rewrap his only son around my finger with a brand new Xbox; money can't buy love, but it can buy time—I guess I always knew mine would run out. Nonetheless, I appropriately pulled up behind Wes's car. He immediately jumped out—door left wide open as presumed. But before I could follow his lead, I gawked at my own wary reflection in the car mirror. I saw myself for the first time, clearer than a leafless sunset. I took a long beat before exiting the vehicle, filling my lungs with a deep sigh of defeat; I realized there's no one I'd leave a car door opened for.

Wes lost his shit when I approached, already holding Brookes protectively in his arms. He hadn't said a word but had a crazed look in his crisp blue eyes. At that moment, I felt the first gust of an autumn breeze cut through the thick, late-summer air. The dogs howled with the wind, pounding their giant heads against the battered fence as I coiled back in fear, ready to make a run for it. But Wes didn't flinch. I swear if he didn't have that sweaty child heaving into his shoulder blade, he probably would've killed me right there. Before we knew it, the dog owners—an old couple looking like the smell of mothballs—ran over to console the beasts, glaring ahead at us as if we were the ones barking. Wes—scarily cold and stoic—turned from me to the neighbors, as if he was uncertain to whom he would lash his insurmountable rage onto first. The neighbors offered tribute, for the old man across from us suddenly softened with familiarity.

"Is that Wesbrooke's boy?" He hollered to Wes with the tinge of a drunken slur. "Oh, your father loved these ol' boys! I'm sure he's smiling down now with the rest of 'em."

As he pointed upwards, I caught the heavenly outline of ten taxidermy Rottweilers, glaring down at us through each windowsill—I knew exactly who we were dealing with now. Wes had given me the full scoop on these ancient wack-a-doos, and, to be fair, I thought he was just being dramatic. Now I felt like a stand-in for *Psycho* Part II, as a giant chill ran up my spine. Why resurrect your goddamn house pets and scare the kids? Oh right, that's because they resurrected their goddamn house pets to scare the "Italians." I must have passed the place a million times—didn't look any less creepy than all of the other forsaken Gilded Age gems around here, including my own. I guess I had just never cared to take a closer look. I half expected to see old Wesbrooke now, standing menacingly beside one of those fluffy, Franken-fucks, looking on at me in final judgment.

Old man Compton, here, chuckled as his fragile wife lurched forward, struggling against the weight of their (living) precious mongrels. Meanwhile, Brookes's blood-curdling screams echoed through the neighborhood.

"I can recall someone just as small being just as afraid!" Mr. Compton teased.

I held my breath as Wes answered him with a steadfast manic stare.

"Come, make Junior pet 'em!" Mr. Compton continued. "A boy's gotta be a man one of these days!"

"OH YEAH? AND WHAT ARE *YOU*, MR. COMPTON?!"

I thought Wes's meltdown would make me look better in Elizabeth's eyes. Yes, I forgot to pick up the kid, but I didn't mouth off at an eighty-year old man. Nonetheless, I sat at the dinner table feeling like a defective puzzle piece; I knew I was supposed to be there, seated at the head of Wes's old table, but I didn't quite fit. The more I tried, the more I dented my edges, as I looked out at the picturesque family, quietly eating dinner beyond me. Maybe this was because Wes placed me there—at the head of the table, I mean. I knew that was my seat but he offered it to me, as if I was a guest stopping by at my own home.

"Hey, babe," I jokingly called to Elizabeth as I sat down. "Remind me to carve my name later, will ya?"

She looked to Wes sharply in reply, as they both scrunched their eyebrows in confusion. So I laughed uncomfortably—like a fucking foreigner trying out American slang for the very first time—and I turned to a ten-year-old to save my dignity. I always wished I had been the one to come up with that name "little old sport;" because that's what he was—just the personage of a quirky, wise old-timer who'd wink and pretend to relate. But this time, his eyes were glazed over, staring into space as if that panic attack earlier shocked his little body and mind into alignment; he was only ten and he now knew it. I suppose we cannot set our own milestones. So without another word, I sat humbly on my ambiguous throne and peered out at the scene before me. I saw everything at this angle … but that was the problem.

After Brookes's unfathomably awkward birthday dinner, Wes pulled out his big, tacky stack of Cuban cigars and cordially invited me for a smoke in my *own* office. I kept my composure despite this indirect blow; the man can throw money on an expensive habit but can barely afford a $25 gift card. And if he thought I was ready for a "stern talking to" to override his manic freak-out, he had another thing coming to him. But that's not what ticked me off most. Rather, it was something about Elizabeth's smile the moment I exited our living room, following her broad-chested peacock of an ex. She looked at us like a doting mother who was just happy her bickering boys were getting along; cue her headshake and modest sip of chardonnay. In that moment, I wanted to pull Wes backwards. We weren't two rowdy brothers, united by camaraderie and our mother's undying love; this was my house, I was the man of it, and I'd lead the way to my own goddamn office.

He was suspiciously interested in everything I had ever done as we sat across from each other in his old leather chairs, drinking whiskey on the rocks and sharing a smoke. The settling warmth of twilight slowly began to darken the room, leaving the antique lanterns to illuminate the mahogany paneled walls. I gave the man what he wanted as I interchangeably puffed my cigar and discussed highlights of my success. It was a good performance he was putting on because I knew it too well from the biz. He wanted to know what he was working with—whom he was up against amidst his failed family unit. He couldn't run a company, but, perhaps, he could salvage an inkling of grace. Maybe we'd become blood brothers while we were at it! There was a sense of satisfaction I was obtaining, as I thought I had him figured out. So I played alongside him, giving him my self-made bullshit story: worked my entire life, left my small town with big ambition and a penny in my pocket—the whole American Dream shebang. He was smitten—absolutely smitten—as he listened keenly, like a child taking mental notes during a father's lecture. Despite his obvious misgivings, the poor guy never realized his own magic. He had a presence; this rare mix of charm and influence that made people turn their heads every time he entered a room. Yet if you told him, he'd ask why they were staring—is there a piece of food on his face?

Is his hair sticking up like Alfalfa's again? And he'd look into your eyes with that sense of earnest innocence that you've been searching for your entire life—in every shifty lover, troubled child, dismissive parent. You'd stare so hard that you'd laugh him off, shaking your head at this illusion of faith. He was one of those people who *could* bounce back but never would.

"You're a lucky guy," Wes started. He was beginning to slur a bit as he gave me that famous crooked side-smile. "You throw yourself in your work but you manage to keep this all together." He gestured to his old home.

"Keep what?"

I wanted to hear him say it.

"I know what you are," He points at me, deflecting my question to my surprise.

I sit up straighter, simultaneously preparing for another showdown and searching for the nearest exit.

"You're like a—like a two-way mirror. No—a two-way bulletproof mirror. No one can see you or even break down the damn thing—not your clients, not your family, not me. You watch us, but you go on with your business. And—and we never see you but we know you're there."

He paused for a beat, taking a last long sip of whiskey. I opened my mouth to defend myself but I wasn't quite sure if I was even being offended. Off my uncertainty, Wes waved his hand in assurance.

"No, no, no! I admire you for it, brother. It's like you only live for something, not—not somebody. You sip your glass half full, but you know when it's empty."

Wes looked out of the window beyond me, as if he caught something running in the dusk-kissed woods. I turned around and came face-to-face with our reflections in the now pitch-black glass.

I couldn't shake this fear that I was asleep—as if I'd nodded off in my hometown's drive-in theater. I'd wake up in a disappointed daze as I glared at the boundless cornfields beyond—the same displaced Midwestern Jew with big dreams already crushed within the oblivion of my even bigger ego. The hick-slut nestled into the crook of my arm would look up at me with big, expectant eyes; she'd say she's Christian and wants to wait—I'd tell her she's Christian so I know she won't. Then I'd push a piece of her hair away, ever so slightly, as I'd tell her everything she wanted to hear. God can't save her but I'm about to. Because in the course of twenty-four hours, she'd be born again into the unfathomable habits of a cold heart. She'd ride the wave of her numbed self, right out of this shanty-town and into the glitz and glamour of Hollywood, where all semi-creative outcasts gather. She'd become one of the top-rated agents, buzzing with the crisp, self-righteous confidence of a *nouveau riche* minority stepping into the limelight. And I'd sit in my local bar with the boys, cackling at an article about her in the daily news; our high school hussy horror stories would surely supersede her success. A girl is only her reputation—past, yet only present if she marries the right schmuck. And that's show business, baby.

Then, that same guy woke up one day and the platinum blonde head lying on the pillow next to him, reeking of alcohol and cheap perfume, matched his empty heart—and that's all the male Joan Didion wrote. But I couldn't pinpoint that feeling quite yet. LA felt like a glitter-filled snow globe; I kept shaking this monotonous piece of glamorous plastic until I didn't care anymore and didn't know what to do with it. So, I put it back down on the table and left. From there, I hopscotched across the map, straight to a famous New York City nightclub to drown out my rootless sorrows at a buddy's bachelor party. Nevertheless, I forgot that it was December—it's real easy to lose track of time when seasons don't exist and you talk to your family on a two-month basis.

As we headed to dinner that first night, I shivered in my borrowed North Face fleece, snow flurries pounding against my bare, balding head, as I eyed passing families; they were all arm-in-arm, braving this bitter weather for window displays and a giant tree. There's nothing worse than Christmas time in this city. Forget waiting for a cab—declared the already-drunken bachelor—the restaurant was a "short" ten-block walk from there. As I fought against snow flurries and the urge to haul my body into moving traffic, I spotted a beautiful woman standing at the corner of the street holding her son. I couldn't tell if she was shaking from the cold or from holding a substantially grown child in her arms.

"You're gonna be waiting a minute there, ma'am," I hooted as I shooed drunk lover boy and the other knuckleheads on ahead. I don't even think I stopped because I cared; I was just curious. It felt like a scene from a movie: young, semi-attractive sleazeball saves out-of-his-league, distraught damsel. That's some Happy Madison Production gold right there.

She held her child protectively, jolting to my abrupt interjection as flurries flew in her fragile face, looking like a perturbed Grace-Kelly-meets-Audrey-Hepburn. I began to feel an unfamiliar pang in my heart, like the Grinch on the verge of saving a commercialized holiday, and immediately regretted hollering at a single-woman on a

New York City street corner. I guess there's always a first.

"Who are you calling 'ma'am'?" She smirked, with a sweet yet endearingly scrappy voice, as her pale, clearly feverish son weakly cranked his head towards the commotion. I respected her good humor in such a bind.

"Let me call a car service for you guys," I pulled my phone out, barely recognizing my own kind words. "It-it's the season for this kind of thing, isn't it?"

"'Tis." The boy's tiny voice corrected.

"Yes, yes, my love," she responded to him. "'Tis the season." She giggled lightly as she took a deep sigh of relief, kissed his forehead, then turned to me. "Thank you, sir."

"Who're you callin' 'sir'?" I smiled. "Don't listen to what they say, we're both too young for that shit—stuff." I corrected. "I'm Joel, Joel Fuchs."

Before she could answer—

"I'm Brookes," the little guy interrupted again, using the last ounce of his energy just to spew a polite introduction. My kinda guy. "Wesbrooke Dodge Ellison IX."

Another pang hits and my icy heart melts.

"Ayy, a swanky name for a swanky little man," I declared holding my cellphone up to my ear.

"A little," he took a deep, tired breath, "old sport."

Then his little head dramatically collapsed onto his mother's shoulder with a tired groan.

"Already got your nose in the classics?! I guess *The Great Gatsby* would make for a solid bedtime tale—slept like a baby in grade school English."

The phone line was busy, so I tried again.

"From Harry Potter to Jay Gatsby; I'm sure my ex-husband wouldn't mind that transition."

She rolled her eyes.

"He rereads that book practically every summer. A Long Island man through and through."

Ex, you say?

"I'm Bit—Elizabeth, by the way."

I gave her my number 'cuz...*why not*? A desperate Long Island divorcée out looking for love; this was one for the books—then adapted for screens, only by the finest of Ventura Agency. And I loved the attention; the key is to give just enough to get *more* back. Upon my return to LA, I concernedly called her to check in, like the good Midwestern gentleman I am. I just *had* to make sure her kid was alright and, well, he wasn't, but she certainly was when I called. Apparently, the poor thing caught pneumonia and would've died if I hadn't sent a car service. I smirked as I pictured her genuinely relieved smile on the other line, thanking me for my kindness; with her divorce, money mess, and Tiny Tim over there, her holiday season was a bust. She quickly apologized for telling me all of this—she didn't know why she just poured her broken heart out to a stranger. Neither did my four coworkers, huddled around the speakerphone, stifling their condescending cackles against former bachelor's air hump brigade.

Over the next three months, Elizabeth and I talked every single day. Well, I talked, and she loyally listened—from work complaints to my daily existential bullshit. Suffice to say, my fifty-minute, ten mile commute—a typical LA minute/mile traffic ratio—was like the therapy session I'd never pay for. She was smart and witty, I'll give her that, but I was most humored by the fact that she had all of this time on her hands for me to waste. Apparently, her newfound freedom—and emergency family trust fund—gave her the power to heal in the way only a financially dependent suburban white woman could: hot yoga, crystals, and spiked kombucha. Meanwhile, I was on my way to pick up Hot Intern from her college on Sunset—remember that platinum blonde I mentioned earlier?

I had Elizabeth on Bluetooth as I waited in front of Hot Intern's campus. She was a budding actress and Boston "model"—hard-Hollywood-seven at best—but I fed her empty ambition with cookie crumbs of praise. She got fat and round with ego by the end of the semester, sprawling her perky body so dutifully across Ventura's casting couch. As Elizabeth rattled on about a MoMa art exhibit, I pictured Hot Intern dramatically descending the front stairs of the building. She'd come down in my favorite red-hot heels, like every other wanna-be Hollywood glamour queen. But this time, I pictured Elizabeth's stunning head on her torso—the woman was twice as old and thrice times more attractive. As I calculated the amount of money Hot Intern would blow to look like her in twenty years, Miss America herself pounded angrily at my $80,000 car's window. I jolted back and instinctively locked my doors. Between Elizabeth's riveting museum review and Bimbo Barbie's bitch fit, I can honestly say I blacked out to the theme song of *Curb Your Enthusiasm.*

"You gave me herpes"—*shrill, unintelligible and unnecessary babbles*— "My dad is a lawyer!"

I sped off with my diseased dick in between my legs, having caught the tail end of the two scariest proclamations in the state of

California.

"What was that?" Elizabeth asked innocently. "I thought I heard knocking?"

"Oh, nothing, just the sound of my pounding heart," I replied with a dramatic sigh, wiping sweat off of my forehead. "I miss you, Elizabeth."

So I schmoozed my way into Elizabeth's understanding heart—thank-her-God for antiviral medication—and out of what would have probably been the start of the #Metoo Movement, with the beauty of corporate hush money and an opening in Ventura's New York City headquarters.

I clench my teeth as the image of Wes, carrying Elizabeth out of his car earlier—like a fucking knight in shining armor—reverberates in my brain. Good job, Wes. Catch her when she's most vulnerable—it takes one to know one. But, at the end of the day, I remember he's got nothin' on us. Elizabeth and I have been one in the eyes of their God for five years now. Bet He thinks Elizabeth Fuchs has a better ring to it too. We talk sometimes—me and the big guy up there—but it's a relatively new relationship and we're easing into it. We're going steady, as the kids no longer say. Tragedy truly brings people together—even the most unlikely pair.

I remember when my dad died. I was fifteen, when mortality doesn't occur to you 'til you see it. Your priorities range from girls, sports, friends, and back to girls; a summer spent at sleep away camp sufficiently hit this pubescent trifecta. It was my first time away and I couldn't have been more excited. I knew my dad was sick, but it was no big deal; he was Dad and he was fine.

As I made my way to the car, hiking pack in tow, a gruff arm tugged me from behind. In one quick swoop, my bags hit the ground and my scrawny body flung over a giant, sweaty shoulder. I choked on my own laughter and the comforting, rank smell of Dad's expensive cologne.

"Go off and do everything I wouldn't do," Dad said, a slight riff in his usual, lovingly ironic tone. Did he jolt a bit when he lifted me?

So I did. Sure, the letters washed in every week; he wanted to hear about it all—every rock jump and baseball game. Did I have my first kiss yet? But I was too busy jumping off rocks, winning games, and kissing girls to respond. The letters became more desperate, yet I continued my childish indifference.

I ended the summer with a ripe tan and a ton of stories to spew at my convenience. I couldn't wait to barge through that front door! I'd wrestle Rex, our Border Collie, as we both sniffed out Dad and raced to his seat in the living room. Instead, Rex was nowhere in sight and I winced at an unfamiliar, pungent smell. My mother, headed down the front stairs with a dingy bathrobe and a distant gaze, jolted at my entry; I probably looked like a ghost through her weary, sunken eyes. People did always say I looked just like my father.

Rex sat at the foot of the quiet, sickly man's bed, his ears perking up for a sign of life instead of the ventilator's teasing gurgle. The rancid smell was antiseptic and perhaps decaying matter; this mysterious man—the antithesis of my two-hundred-pound, rosy-cheeked father—lay on my parents' bed, withering away. A rabbi sat at the man's side, silently reciting prayers in Hebrew. What—this guy thought a few fancy poems were going to be his key to the land of make-believe? I looked forward to chatting with Dad about it later; we'd sit by the front porch and discuss this existential fantasy over cigars again. My mom would yell at him for letting me smoke but I was a man—my bar mitvah papers so proved—and this was what men did, my father confirmed. They didn't quiver at flowery ideologies; they worked hard and lived this short life to the fullest. So his boy was going to smoke a cigar and he was going to damn well like it. It was us against an unforgiving, godless world. And when our time came we'd fall humbly into the abyss; it's where we all came from and where we were all headed, he always said. Nothing could quell the pious atheist. I was sure this guy had a good run—and maybe a week left in him—but why wasn't he with his family? He shouldn't be alone; no one should be alone when they die. My mother stood idly by the bedside, unsure what to do with this stranger, too, as she looked on in silent despair.

My dad always talked about picking up one day, and moving us all to Australia. A land filled with endless summers, no wars, and friendly "discount Brits" humbled by sunlight and political isolation. I wanted to believe that he left without us—ran off to paradise without an explanation. I couldn't understand how a man like my father, with his sharp cynicism and derisive humor, couldn't outwit the grim reaper. But he lay there in surrender, reciting the rabbi's prayers with a warm, content smile planted on his sunken face. Suddenly, he reached his arm past the rabbi, readying a handshake for an invisible acquaintance beyond. Even in that moment, I never thought I'd start reaching.

I curiously reached across Brookes's desk for a small, clear baggie, so "cleverly" hidden directly behind his pencil sharpener. I shook my head at the familiar white substance in the palm of my hands—I really thought kids were sneakier these days. So I wanted to believe that this was some kind of a hoax. I wanted to believe that that smart-ass sitting in my office four years ago really knew better than I—and the rest of them. But why should he? We've all been there—I was an LA bachelor in the '80s, for crying out loud—and had the time of our lives. Summer nights, riding one-hundy down the Pacific Coast Highway in a blue Corvette, engine roaring in alignment with Steven Tyler's iconic screams bumping from the speakers. The night is yours, this life is yours, and you realize you probably didn't need drugs to reach this euphoric high. But you did it anyway. There are a lot of things we don't have to do when we're young—but we do it all anyway. Yet we hear, see, and experience the warning signs before us. Mom tells you about the eighteen-year-old Harvard kid whom she read about in the paper—he took laced drugs; your childhood best friend hangs on life support after a drunk driving accident; a quiet class bookworm commits suicide. Unfortunately, we are all signs of our times. We are the heartbroken music lyrics, the racy movie scenes, the misguided media posts. We secretly place our ear buds in when Mom talks; we drink our sorrows away to commemorate the fallen, because we, ourselves, are falling; we post on social media, knowing the reaction though surprised at the outcome. Rich, poor, middle class—everyone has a narrative. We write down our stories, dreams, delusions, in our minds, like secret essays—because if we read them aloud, we'll expose ourselves. We'll mock the vigor of youth. So I placed the baggie back where I found it. Me and God— excuse me, God and I—have been tight ever since.

"SHUT UP! JUST SHUT UP!" Elizabeth stands up from her seat and hollers ahead.

I laugh uncontrollably.

PART IV:

THE WASP AT THE FUNERAL

I could stand at the podium and say that I, Wesbrooke Dodge Ellison IX—known affectionately as Brookes—am in Heaven. A land of eternal blue skies overlooking boundless flower fields—prettier than a PC screensaver. I race deceased relatives through tickless grass as we fall onto a pile of roses—no thorns, no worries. We're giddy, loved, and safe within an eternity of ignorant bliss. We have what we want *and* what we need in this Place, like a Marxist society on FDA-approved crack. I could stand at the podium and say that I, Brookes—cheekily known as junior, more to commemorate my dad's favorite HBO show than his own namesake—am in Hell. Life's temptations gave my young soul a run for God's money and I simmer in a layer of fiery embers with the worst of them. So I high five Hitler and creep back into the shadows from whence I came.

Nah, I won't say all of that. I mean, what would you say at your own damn funeral? Don't act like you've never thought about it. You'd stand at the podium and scale the crowd, counting your followers faster than your blessings. But I'm up here, primed and ready to spit some spiritually enlightened, Hakuna-Matata fire for you people anyway, because—*buzzz*. I choke on my lost words and peer around embarrassingly as if I slipped into a stutter. Not that it even matters.

I know I'm dead … but I still *feel* human—now, more so than ever. You'd think that I woulda finally found the right words—that I'd have a voice up here. I check my hands—just in case—but they're mine through and through. No bee wings—no sticky insect claws. Shitty karmic reincarnation cannot be the answer to this. So I take a breath, and try again. This time, I'll start us off with a nice quote: "Love is patient, love is kind—" *Buzzzzzzzzzzzzz*. I look to the floor, feeling my face grow hot with frustration.

I stood there, staring ahead through bleary, squinting eyes, at my giggling third grade class. Today was "hero day." Green Vale was one of those elementary prep schools that made a mountain out of a molehill for milestone events—this was our first "grade school" presentation. So, they threw us in monkey-suits, rallied the yearbook photographer, invited the school's headmaster—where was Long Island's finest (and dare I say, hottest) *News 12* anchor? Anyway, each of us had to pick a living hero, write an essay, and recite it, by memory, to the entire class—and of course, our heroes. In a world of Super-mans and Spider-Mans, we all picked our dads by default.

But I really thought Dad *was* Batman. "Bruce Wayne" was just a fictionalized front for *the* Wesbrooke Dodge Ellison, of Ellison Manor, he'd proclaim. This was easy to believe—we did, in fact, live in a mansion, and Dad looked like a cheekier Michael Keaton, circa Burton's *Batman*. Dad sat humbly in his high-end suit of armor, ready to zoom off through the mean streets of the New York Stock Exchange. Anytime now, he'd be gone—and I'd be here. Most businessmen put their hearts and souls into their careers. Mine didn't and maybe that was the problem; he had his heart in a billion-dollar venture and a soul for us to keep. Unfortunately, that's not how it works—no matter how hard he tried.

I shake my head and laugh at this memory; personal anecdotes are key—yet we'll just as quickly throw its dangling chain up in the air and swallow it whole, like a cartoon character locking away a nemesis. And we relate to them in a way, for these villains always return. But we're not cartoons. If we swallow a key, we will surely shit it out. And with that, I stand at my funeral podium and say, that "out beyond ideas of wrongdoing and rightdoing, there is a field. I'll meet you there." When we do, we'll have a toss—I'll bring a football, there should be one somewhere around this Place. *Back and forth, back and forth* until we tire, and "when the soul lies down in that grass, the world is too full to talk about." Then I'll ask you all to meet us there, and lie down.

I straighten up—chin out, shoulders back—I am a Child of God; I am an Awakened One; I am a Prophetic Believer. I am all that's out there and more in the projections of the loved ones and acquaintances ahead—a solid turnout, if I do say so myself. I see them clear as day. In their eyes, my young body amounted to nothing. In their hearts, my ever-present soul has attained everything. But have you ever listened to your heart before? I don't mean in a cheesy way, like saying what you mean or choosing grapefruit over black cherry White Claw—you serial killer, you. What I mean is: have you ever actually listened to your heart—like a doctor with a stethoscope or a meditating monk? If you focus hard enough, everything and everyone around you becomes a low rumble; you finally hear yourself over the noise. But it's—

"Tough. That's just tough." Dad would sigh in mock-seriousness.

"What's tough?" I'd ask in excited anticipation.

"Life."

"What's Life?*"*

"A magazine."

"Where'd ya get it?"

"CVS."

"How much?"

"10 dollars. How much you got?"

"Five."

"That's tough."

"What's tough?"

"Life."

"What's Life?*"*

"A game."

"Where'd ya—wait, no it's not, daddy. It's a magazine!"

"That's tough." He'd poke.

"What's tough?" I'd smirk.

"Life."

"What's Life?*"*

"I heard it was a magazine."

"Where'd ya get it?"

"CVS."

"How much it cost?"

A life.

Today, I refused to wear my new glasses. Dad claimed they reeked of "European nobility"—whatever that meant—and gave our legacy of caped crusaders a run for our money. First of all, life is about timing, old man, and these little assholes sitting in front of me, read *Harry Potter* like it was the toddler *Bible*. Sure, I was generally the class clown and my parents' daily dinner-party muse. So normally, I'd take my classmates' jeers, mold them into my next act, and walk around as if I held some sort of precedence over them all. But last night, Batman took off his mask and revealed the eyes of a total stranger. I pounded and pounded on that Batcave door, because Dad had to be in there somewhere. I didn't need a super hero anymore.

Suddenly, the cameras flashed, kids laughed, and I totally blacked out. Fast forward to the school hallway. Dad knelt beside me, as I stared down at the world crumbling beneath my tiny, leather-shoed feet. I felt out of my body—head pounding, heart skyrocketing, as if I had been swooped from an undertow.

"What happened out there?" Dad asked calmly.

Silence.

"I think I know," he responded dramatically. "I can't believe it! You almost revealed my secret identity, little old sport!"

I shyly matched his crooked grin.

Who, where, what am I now? I throw my hands up ironically at you all—even to you, dear reader—I see you in this crowd. Am I Big Brother looming? Did technology find a way to digitally synchronize our souls to the world after we've physically left it? Does the government know and there's something they're not telling us? They've hired Bill Gates to speak "code" to space aliens as they trade our souls for intergalactic peace between the wider universe and this thumbnail of an existence we call Earth, making our end simply the beginning of alien slavery? IS IT ALL A SIMULATION?

I scared you there, didn't I? Well, relax, because I don't have your answers and I won't humor yours. If you love me, please do not wish me in Heaven. If you hate me, please do not damn me to Hell. I'm not here and I'm not over there—wherever "there" is. Let me exist in my absence. Let me be Elsewhere. Or just call it that Place I mentioned before. Now, I bet you think I'm some omnipotent, omniscient force; perhaps I'm about to release final judgment on our previous narrators as I divulge each family member's torturous truth. But, truth lies in the bullshit of the beholder—including yours truly. And you, yourself, you goddamn human being. So, finish this tale … and come to no conclusions.

Or, make them up as you go. I'm not here to tell you how to live your life. But, thank you for sitting here before me today to understand mine; maybe people don't go to funerals to mourn, they go to understand. They wanna know what this hereafter stuff is all about as they create romance out of eternal longing and the heartache of human disconnection. The Anglo-Saxons created Beowulf; Mark Zuckerberg invented Facebook. But I am not all-powerful—I won't haunt or bless you with my presence; I am not all-knowing—I promise there's wisdom in insecurity. I am this moment—and you wanna know something? I'm alright.

But that quote—it was a good one, wasn't it? I could've kept going with that Corinthians proverb, but we're at a funeral, not a wedding here. I guess some people might compare the two—the death of a man and the death of a man's libido. But, hey, that's just another set of adult problems I'm glad I'll never have to deal with. A decent quote *and* a dead-boy quip—I'm on a roll today, ladies and gentlemen.

And I always loved a good audience. Every night for an entire month, my living room was my stage and my wine-drunk parents were my biggest fans. Their standing ovations would surely ring beyond those four mahogany walls to the hearts of all. I totally had *Peter Pan* in the bag. Well, I didn't, and like any good only-child, I was upset, and I made sure everyone knew it. Green Vale was small; when one kid acted out, every student, teacher, parent—and perhaps even the janitor—had you on their radar. Problem children do not exist at The Green Vale School. Pupils soar from nursery to ninth grade in perfect harmony with themselves and the demands of higher elementary education. With their Latin motto, "Optima Durant" (The Best Endures) branded on our ass like cattle, everyone was watching and waiting to buzz about the next kid who couldn't take the burn. According to our school psychologist, I merely had a case of "only child misdirected rage syndrome." This expert diagnosis would entail a daily dose of attention and "an outlet for my artist's heart." So, Mom booked me acting classes in one of the most exclusive studios in the city.

Instead, Dad and I went on a hunting trip to the Adirondacks. As we drove along, it was an hour in and we had to pee. We took the next exit to Woodstock, New York—Dad wanted to see if hippies used bathrooms or bushes. Naturally, this chirp flew over my seven-year-old head. However, the thought of peeing in a bush as opposed to a relegated space just added to my excitement for this father-son weekend. Initially, mom had juiced up my acting-bug ego, enough for me to believe that I would take over Hollywood with the twinkle of my baby blues and the swoon of my crooked smize. I was gonna "show them" after my *Peter Pan* fail ... then, I didn't.

"I'm never gonna be the next Mally Culkin, Daddy," I whined, lip trembling on the verge of a tantrum.

Dad quelled this quick—otherwise, this would be a long trip.

"It's Macaulay Culkin, little old sport—and please, don't."

Poor guy grew up to be a crackhead or something.

"Be the next Brookes Ellison—the one and only. How 'bout that?"

We laughed together as he pulled my new, gigantic coon hat over my eyes.

As we pulled into town, I felt like I was entering a whole new world. Rock band posters hung from store windows; men wore their long hair over ragged tie-dye tees; music blared along the sidewalks. I thought this all only existed in movies, or another era. I was intrigued.

"Why are those posters so bright, Daddy?" I asked quizzically.

"Psychedelic traffic signs," he answered matter-of-factly.

"Can't their moms take them for a haircut?"

"They weren't hugged as a child."

"Why's that music so loud?"

"So God can hear."

"What's that weird smell?"

Dad suddenly sniffed the air, suspicious squints darting around the car.

"Brooksey," he sneered, in his best Mr. Krabs impression. "I think you smell a smelly smell—"

Any dads out there, quoting *Spongebob* to placate your kids ...

you guys deserve a gold medal.

I smirked as I finished it off—

"That smells … SMELLLLLY!"

We cackled heartily as I beat my tiny feet on the dashboard.

"And that's all you need to know for now, little old sport."

As I waited for Dad outside the public bathroom—update: hippies do in fact use sanitary means of relieving themselves—I sharply paced to and fro, looking like *G. I. Joe* Elmer Fudd; a seven-year-old must humor himself within the catastrophically long three minutes it takes for a grown man to pee. At my last turn, I noticed a whiteboard hanging on the wall high above me. A pen dangled from it on a string next to indecipherable, blurry writing. I smiled mischievously as I stood on my tippy toes and successfully made my chicken scratch mark: BROOKES WAS HERE.

"Well, I guess we didn't need a bush to mark our territory," Dad laughed, scooping me up in arms.

Even at eye level, I knew I couldn't read those words—but no one else did. In Mrs. Corrigan's professional opinion—Green Vale's beloved forty-yearer—I was simply a slow reader. This woman had one foot in the classroom and the other in a nursing home; however, my parents paid $10k of my year's tuition for me to participate in a separate reading enrichment program—Green Vale's version of special ed—as I stealthily hid my squints.

"Read this quote to me, bud," he was onto me. "It's a good one!"

I looked like Zoolander as I attempted my best neutral, inconspicuous squint, before habitually hiding in the crook of his neck.

"So, that's what it's been this whole time," he shook his head, more at the situation than the bamboozler in his arms. "Mrs. Corrigan, you old fuckin' bat—"

I gasped at his cuss.

"Ay, ay!" He said in his best mobster voice. "Add it to the cursing jar, joon-ya. Or, just … FUGGEDABOUTIT!"

We giggled together.

"Hmm, so I guess this big adventure calls for a big, new look! There must be an eye glass store around here somewhere—"

"Nooooooo!" I cried.

I wouldn't give in!

"John Lennon wears glasses! Remember that song 'Hey Jude?'? You loved it! That's him!

"Soooooooooo?!" I howled.

"Wow, tough crowd, tough crowd. Well, I'll have you know, our great American president, Teddy Roosevelt donned a pair at every hunting outing—"

"Grandpa hated him!"

This world leader had the audacity to attempt regulating and upending American royalty, before the fall of '29 could do it. Grandpa had thoughts.

"Grandpa hated everybody!" He retorted with a splash of ingrained disdain.

Also true.

"But our fine, romantic poet Rumi here—" he gestured to the whiteboard, as he began reading, "once said, 'Out beyond ideas of wrongdoing and right-doing, there is a field. I'll meet you there. And when the soul lies down in that grass, the world is too full to talk about.' But you can't talk about it if you can't see it, little old sport!"

I took a contemplative beat.

"Fuggedaboutit, Daddy."

Sit there, my peers, family, strangers alike, and dwell on your own mortality, as I reel us back to the human heart. They lie dormant within us, hidden beneath layers of our existence—skin, flesh, bone— like Russian dolls. Look around now—we have this stuffy room, beyond that we have sprawling earth; look further to colossal skies … trek deeper for space. Every night, a shining, mysterious moon beams down from there as our only proof of galaxies beyond—of the unknown. We may not fully reach it in our lifetime, but we'll always feel the presence of its light. Find me there. *Rocketmannnnnnnnn, burning up his fuse up here alone …* Sorry—I had to.

"I heard it! There's something in there!" I hollered to poor groggy Mom as she peered into my bedroom closet.

"There's no one in here, honey."

"Can we read *Harry* again? I can't sleep."

"Brookes, you know it's time."

"I can't, Mommy—it's a full moon. All the weirdos are out!"

"And perhaps the Sanderson Sisters?" she replied disapprovingly, as she found the root of my Halloween night terrors.

On cue, Dad popped his head in the doorway, illuminating the dark room with the light of a match and his goofy grin.

"Oh Brooksey, it's all just a bunch of—" He whipped out a long white candle. "Hocus pocus!"

I screamed as he lit it—half amused, half horrified, as I dove into my pillow.

"What did I say about scary movies before bed, Wesbrooke?" she scolded.

"Which one?" Dad asked, and will always ask, in the same doofy surprise, until the day he reaches his own fuckin' funeral podium.

"The one who doesn't beat a dead polo pony into the ground, little old sport!" I thought I heard Grandpa spew, beyond the crypt.

"What? It's just Disney Channel!" Dad countered innocently, turning over to me in his Batman voice. "Disney Channel's *31 days of Fright Fest!*"

"Those movies are far too scary for him. You know this! That's it—I'm setting up those parental controls—"

"Come on!" Dad and I wined in unison as I peered up from my pillow.

"Fine," Mom glared at dad in annoyance. "Then *you* will handle thirty-one days of sleepless nights, my dear." She strutted out of the room, nose in the air.

Dad shrugged before playfully lurking over toward me, back hunched over like Nosferatu, as his spooky, candlelit shadow crawled across my wallpaper.

"I want Mom." I quickly dove back into my pillow.

I gotta say, a boy needs his mom. There's this sense of—of—I peer over to my mom ahead. As her vacant eyes stare past me, a shiver runs up my spine. I clutch the podium for support. So, I guess that's just it. A mother's love it's—it's—

I lay on my belly, *Pokémon* nightshirt pulled up, as mom gently caressed my tiny torso. *Warm.* Warmth rose up my vertebrae, gracefully skimmed my cranium, and finally seeped into my restless mind. Meanwhile, my mouth hung loose in a trance as I fought my drooping lids. I couldn't fall asleep yet—I had to keep an eye out for witches flying across the autumn moon.

"Okay, doll. Now it's time—" she said soothingly, as she slowly tugged down my shirt.

"Nooo, don't goooo!" I managed to protest in my exhausted stupor. "Moon … full—full moon, Mommy!"

Mom sighed, laughing lightly and maintaining the patience of a saint. I was sure a pain in the ass—

"But you're my pain," she'd always add.

"You know, when I was a little girl, Wesbrooke, I loved nights like this. I'd tiptoe to my window," she improvised, as she made her way over to the sill, looking out at the old oaks casting dreamy, mysterious shadows against the moonlit grass. "and look out for fairies dancing in the light."

"No monsters or witches?" I interjected.

"None. But I didn't want to scare the fairies away, so I'd peer out," she cautiously moved forward, "then—quick!" and pulled away just as the moonlight caught her.

"But I'd always miss them," her smile fell slightly, as she inched closer again, like a shy child checking one last time. "Before I moved from my childhood home, I tried to take a picture of the woods in my yard on a night like this."

"Why?"

"I don't know, doll. I guess I just wanted to capture the fairies."

"Can you sing to me?" I continued to stall.

She pattered over and laid beside me, leaning on her elbow for support.

"Hmm let's try my favorite oldie …" she yawned, taking a moment to recollect, as she rubbed my forehead in hypnotic circles.

"On the day that you were born, the angels got together and

decided to create a dream come true. So they sprinkled moon dust in your hair of gold and starlight in your eyes of blue!"

"I like this." I approved, as I folded my little hands across my chest.

"That is why all the girls in town—or boys," she added, oh-so-progressively, *"Follow you all around just like me, they long to be close to you."*

I gently opened my eyes to catch her melancholic smile, half glowing in the soft, natural light, half hidden in the dark—like the beginning of a rare eclipse.

I pause for a moment and take a look at each patron as I gage the fine line drawn between care and curiosity. Joel was right—people *are* art. They are portraits in a gallery, each meshing into the next until you take a closer look and pretend to care—not a big museum guy. But in this moment, I'm a careful curator:

"How did he really die?" howls *The Scream.*

"His mother is so strong and collected," *Mona Lisa* murmurs.

"They all just seem so complacent and meek," declares *the Girl with a Pearl Earring.*

"Is someone even going to speak?" whines one-eared Van Gogh.

It was my tenth birthday and Joel wouldn't shut the fuck up. At our family dinner table, I was usually the talker. I had stories to tell—some true, most elaborated—and I didn't appreciate anyone stealing my thunder. One day, Dad moved out, and this loud, fast-talking Hollywood dude moved in. I couldn't tell if I liked Joel or not. He was funny but I didn't understand his jokes; he was smart but asked me intrusive questions. So, I'd laugh, nod and go along with whatever he said, because that's what kids do—especially if you hand them the newest Xbox—until you make them grow up.

I faintly remember meeting Joel. Me and Mom were in Manhattan to see *The Nutcracker* when, halfway through, I found myself dozing in and out. As a costumed rat danced across the stage, my head grew weary, eyelids drooping, and I thought I was finally dying of boredom. Instead, I had a one hundred three degree fever. In my flu-ridden daze, I woke up to the pounding of bitter snow flurries, and the sight of a balding Jewish man flirting with my mother. Suddenly, Dad's last words rang in my head.

"Lastly," Dad relayed in a quick, stern whisper, standing at our front door with his suitcase in hand, as generations of Ellison men turned in their graves.

"You're the man of the house now, little old sport. Keep your mother safe and a firm shake." He demonstrated, direct eye contact and all. "You never know who you'll need to scare."

I tried in that moment—as intimidating as a flu-ridden seven-year old could be—but Joel came back intact … less hair, but all there.

At least he had decent book taste. Mom annoyingly monitored my TV and video game intake growing up; she wanted me to use "my imagination," but at this point, I was too old to play with action figures, too ADD for Legos, and too lazy to learn an instrument. I was bored and getting an attitude about it all. If Joel had any real say, I would've watched TV until my eyes dried out. Then he'd have Mom all to himself. Instead, he showed me the magic of books—I couldn't watch TV but I could read *any* book—*"skies the limit,"* he'd say. It was like binge watching On Demand; you scored through some classics, dabbled in comedies, and watched more pay-per-view than you'd care to admit. And my school nurtured these scholarly habits, so I knew I wouldn't get my ass kicked. I wasn't into censored, child-friendly mysteries or watered down adventures; I wanted the thrill of a real narrative. I wanted the truth. Joel and I practically had our own book club throughout elementary school. We'd buy books together, he'd lecture me on new vocabulary, explain innuendos I couldn't quite grasp—and probably wasn't ready to—and just generally tried to be the father he thought I should have. There was so much going on beyond this tiny, quaint existence here on Long Island. The world was imperfect—it was scary, dirty, unforgiving. And I was to be the next president, Bill Gates, Jeff Bezos, Wolfgang Amadeus Mozart—

But it takes a village to make a monster, from the clay of its own soil. If we don't follow the rules, we won't be something ... it's not that we won't live our lives—no—it's more that our lives won't live on. Yet, sometimes—only sometimes—you look around and find yourself within the heat of your own madness. If and when you get there, reader: shrug, kick back, and light that shit on fire.

I wandered aimlessly around my local library. Well, not *that* local—I would go to the one in Sea Cliff, a small, nearby town along the water. "Sea," "cliff." Get it? Anyway, it was close enough to bike but far enough to avoid people—because *everyone* is hanging out at the library during holiday breaks. We were all home for Easter, to celebrate the rise of Christ and our final spring break. After ninth grade, all twelve or so kids that were left in the class (most students who stay home for high school, leave and endure a real freshmen year) went our separate ways to some of the best boarding schools across New England. But we'd always make time to catch up—we were honorary siblings, thrown together at Green Vale before we could talk. Whether at school or country club events, we learned to like each other. Tonight, we all planned to meet at our favorite towny hole-in-the-wall, a shanty fun-to-hate bar sitting along the Long Island Sound called Wall's Wharf. This last hurrah was predictable to say the least. It was college acceptance season, and I knew they'd wave those Ivy League letters around like the American flag. I didn't tell them yet, but *"this is how they do it in Europe, guys"*—I pictured myself confidently spewing—*"gap years are the norm there. What can I say; I'm a worldly man."* Then I'd give 'em that ol' crooked grin, and, somehow, everything would be okay.

I strolled further down until I found myself on the opposite end of the American author alphabet, mindlessly running my fingers over each title. I paused as I spotted big, bold, red letters: *On the Road.* Joel recommended this one to me a while back. I was twelve, so Jack Kerouac's jumpy free verse, and beatnik spirit, read like Mandarin. Now, with my new post grad plans, I never felt closer to this '50s hipster-guru. The novel dives into Kerouac's cross country, existential escapades, as he searches for the pursuit of happiness in the form of adventure, bottomless beer bottles, and beautiful women—damn, did I copy that off of SparkNotes? So, I thought I'd give him another chance, instead of making Joel pay for four more years of wasted higher education. But I knew referencing even a single remnant of our failed bromantic past would be key. I most definitely had to get a few pages in before later; you can't bullshit a bullshitter—but you can try.

I walloped through our front door, ready to fly to my room,

swallow a monster bong rip, and avoid my inevitable college talk until dinnertime. I approximate a fifteen minute lecture, a five minute self-righteous Joel rant, and an hourlong private "co-parent" scheme to save my plunging fate. This gave me substantial time to digest my food, nap, prepare for the night, and dip out through the maid quarters. However, just as I felt our ancient staircase creak beneath my cyclops feet, I spotted a fat envelope with my name on it sitting on our entry hall table. The letter was from Harvard. But ... I didn't even apply.

I paced around our main hall bathroom—*back and forth, back and forth*—desperately trying to control my short, angry breaths. Suddenly, the room got smaller, my heart grew louder—shit, it was happening again. I practically tore the medicine cabinet off its hinges. Mom never sleeps, Joel fakes back pain: bop it, twist it ... crush it ... mix it ... and you're Batman again.

"'The only people for me are the mad ones!'" I barked at Joel, high out of my mind during dinner, as I quoted a famous excerpt from *On the Road.* "'The ones who are mad to live, mad to talk, mad to be saved, desirous of everything at the same time—'"

Joel threw his hands up.

"What is this—a quote from the fuckin' *Dead Poet's Society?* Gimme a break, drama king."

"'The ones who never yawn—'" I continued, beaming with Ellison mania, as if my grandfather's melodrama came rushing to the surface, "'or say a commonplace thing, but burn, burn, burn like fabulous yellow roman candles exploding like spiders across the stars in the middle you see the blue center light pop and everybody goes—'"

"Awww!" Slurred some random South Shore girl at the bar, her Long Island accent as thick and aggressive as her perfume. "So, Harvard?!"

Her big eyes bulged behind dark eyeliner, like a doe-eyed raccoon.

"That's like fuckin' AWH-SOME!"

As I pondered how trash *does* occasionally wash up on Wall's Wharf's rocky bay, I quickly checked myself: *Got a lotta' say, little old snob. You're declining Harvard and this poor girl clearly just wants a free bee*r.

Bartender Deb—not Deborah, just Deb—a hot, middle-aged MILF, leaned her perky boobs atop the shipwreck-themed-tavern's counter, as she handed over some pens. No I.D.'s, no problem, as my friends confidently signed their parents' credit card checks.

South Shore girl confusedly eyed my empty hand.

I turned away.

Unfortunately, I was the DD tonight and there's nothing worse than being sober—look, it's all perspective—at Wall's. Everyone around you is sloshed, and you feel like the fucking "Piano Man," ready to pull out your harmonica and ironically relate to blue-collar America. But you see *everything* at this level, as I begin eavesdropping on a fat drunk debutante and her old Green Vale classmate; she's a twenty-four year old virgin and has been hiding behind money and Catholicism since anyone can remember. I catch her hungrily eyeing a half-eaten nacho platter as if its gonna run off the plate and take her chastity with it. Meanwhile, this guy was sufficiently drunk, and she was a soft six in this bar's gritty, unforgiving lighting—good enough for him. Because those fluorescent bulbs, also caught a dazzling rock nestled on a lean, dainty hand across the bar; this future Long Island housewife looked offensively happy without him, as she threw a polite, contemptless wave. There was no way this guy was going home alone tonight. I chuckled before turning to the next couple, hoping to be as equally entertained in my faded reverie—but it was the same two people ... then the same ... then more of the same, duplicated across the bar. Their eyes on the same platter ... looking around for that same ex ... Damn. I was spooked. But I laughed to myself—and all of them for that matter. They'd all wake up next to a fat virgin and a bitter dumpee.

But Deb would serve them until they'd forget. She rinsed a beer glass for her next customer, looking on at me curiously as my subconscious mind crash-landed back into this hallowed shithole.

"You okay, kid?" She asked suspiciously in her raspy— surprisingly sexy—local tongue.

I straightened up, broadening my scrawny chest as she laughed.

"Wait, you look just like him—yaw Wes's boy!"

My friends, in earshot, stifled condescending cackles to one another.

"He was a regula here!" She continued in oblivion. "How's he been?"

Well, his isolated 'cottage out east,' took the form of a 'temporary retreat' then became a rehab for the rich elite. He's doing his best, Deb.

"Your guess is as good as mine," I answered.

My friends howled. I joined them. And this is how teenage boys laugh past the pain.

South Shore girl's tits grazed my fleece, reverting back my attention, as Deb made her rounds. So I humored the girl and ordered a drink already—for myself. I wasn't *that* nice.

"So where are you headed this fall?" I boredly inquired.

"UNF."

Her shoulders slacked as Deb handed me my tab.

"Hm?"

"University of North Florida."

Florida? Why, of course.

"Cool. What high school did you go to?" I planned to play twenty awkward one answer questions until she'd bore, and move on.

"Seaford. You know anyone from there?" She began twirling her scrunched, wet-looking curls.

The Florida of Long Island?

"Nah, but I've heard of the town."

"Well, duh! Where you from?"

"Glen Cove—"

"No way! I, like, actually know a few people from—"

"But went to Green Vale." I quickly corrected.

"Oh!" Her eyes lit up like a human light bulb. My prestige gained me an unwarranted college legacy acceptance and a potential post-game blowjob—I may be dead, but I didn't die a saint.

"Green Vale, then boarding school after ninth—out in Massachusetts. You probably wouldn't know it."

She nodded in compliant agreement, feeling a little dumber yet inching a little closer. Girls love a good asshole—my stepfather had proved—so I'd be nice. I'd be honest. I'd be myself. And hopefully she'd skulk off until further notice.

"Hey, I have a random question," I looked on at her now in earnestness.

"Lay it on me!" She winked.

"If we went home together tonight," I began, "and I died … Would you go to my funeral?"

"Umm, like, what?" She giggled nervously, her spray-tanned nose scrunched in confusion.

"If we fucked," I reiterated slowly. "and I dropped dead tonight … Would you go to my funeral?"

"You're a freak!" She playfully joked, simultaneously weirded out and wanting me. Girls love a good closet asshole—*Joel grasps my mom's hand ahead. I cringe.*

"Well, think about it," I offered, "If you say no, than you're a bitch. But, if you say yes, than you're a weirdo."

She never answered my question. Nevertheless, she hopped in the backseat of Dad's beat-up Mercedes, squishing between about five or so of my plastered friends. We sped over Bayville Bridge and along West Shore Road, windows down, breathing in the familiar low-tide of the Long Island Sound beside us. The guys annoyingly squabbled with my staticky radio, but I ignored them, and peacefully eyed the glow of the moon against the calm, still water. To my right, sat old, grotesque manors, lost in the night's dark shadows. I looked back to the road, too aware of the contrasting forces lurking within my peripherals. Suddenly, a spark lit under me, as I jerkily smacked my friends, and popped in a cassette (yeah, the car was *that* old), to everyone's annoyance.

We are graced with a guitar introduction then—*old maaan, look at my life*—Neil Young crooned—*I'm a lot like you were.*

"Nawww, come on!" someone complained.

"Turn this shit off, man!"

"Not now, Potter—"

We get another guitar break, then—

"*Old maaaaaan, look at my life,*" I shamelessly spewed, with a content smile, as I flashed back to me and Dad's last road trip.

"*Twenty-four and there's so much more,*" Dad sang loud and proud in the car, as my big, innocent eyes peered up at him from under my coon hat. "*Live alone in a paradise, that makes me think of two.*"

"*Love lost,*" South Shore girl brought me back, looking cuter by the minute in my rearview, "*Such a cost.*"

I helped her out: "*Give me things that don't get lost, like a coin that won't get tossed, rolling home to you.*"

My friends contentedly bopped their heads now, finally settling the fuck down.

Cue the tight banjo-guitar-riff … I blast my speakers … then—

"*OLD MAN TAKE A LOOK AT MY LIFE,*" we all sing, "*I'M A LOT LIKE YOU, IIIIIIIIIII NEED SOMEONE TO LOVE ME THE WHOLE DAY THROUGH ! AHHH, ONE LOOK IN MY EYES—*"

Tears stream down Dad's face …

"*AND YOU CAN TELL THAT'S TRUE!*"

As I pulled into my circular driveway, I eyed the ancient lanterns along the house, lit proudly as if nothing and no one would ever dim their lights. All felt right. This is home. I walked through my front door met by a cold draft breezing from a window across the hall. We never could get those old, stiff windows to open—why the hell did Joel bother with them tonight? Suddenly Mom walked past me, holding a hot cup of chamomile, as she concernedly eyed the window beside the front door.

"Oh, uh, just dropped off soma' the guys," I stuttered, in an attempt to look and sound as sober as possible, "I DDed tonight."

She looked past me with a passive aggressive pout, as she stopped in the middle of the hall, shaking her head in disappointment.

I shivered.

"Come on, Mom, it's not that late. I shouldn't even have a curfew—I'm about to graduate!"

She massaged her temples, getting more quietly aggravated by the second.

"Okay, I'm sorry." I softened, as I ran up to her, shameful tears flooding my eyes.

I leaned in for a hug; no matter how mad she was, she'd never— she walked away as I approached, heading up the steps.

Did my hand just graze her arm—or pass through it?

"I said I'm sorry," my voice shook anxiously, "Mom, come on—"

She kept walking.

"Listen to me, Mom, I'm sorry. I said I'm sorry!"

She stopped to sip her tea.

"Mom—*buzzz*." This obscene sound flew out from my mouth, like a demonic possession.

I tried again.

"M—*buzzzzzzzzzzzzz*."

I stare at the two portraits sitting atop my own closed casket. I want them to remember me like this—alive on the surface, with color, energy, and vibrancy—even though I'm dead underneath. I touch my most recent picture and leave a nice, grimy fingerprint on its glass enclosure.

"Lookin' good Wesbr—"

Buzzzzzzzzzzzzzzzzzzzzzzzzzzzzzzzzzzzzzzzzzzzzzzzzzzzzzzzzzzzzzzzzzzzzzzzzzzzzzzzzzzzzzz.

I instinctively turn to the funeral patrons, as if I had signaled an alarm, with my own malformed words. No one noticed—but I always thought people peeled their sights on the dead. They seek signs, omens—anything for us to let them know we're there. Yet, they clasp their hands in prayer, eyes shut tight for clarity ... forever blinded by their own faith.

But Mom stares right at me now in horror, as she rises from her seat.

"SHUT UP! JUST SHUT UP!" She screams at me.

... Perhaps she screamed *to* me. I confidently rise back to the podium, as I realize, she screamed *for* me.

THE END.

Made in the USA
Columbia, SC
17 March 2023

a5ba1d8e-f26c-4d0b-86f8-bd3e098770b7R01